C C S

by Tagenar

Cover art by **Buggy** aka. **ReezyTheGarchomp**, furaffinity.net/user/reezythegarchomp/

Editing by **Al Song**, furaffinity.net/user/alsong/

Published by KTM Publishing

Print edition set in Fanwood and Akashi, both royalty-free typefaces

Print edition ISBN: 978-1-7322824-6-9

1

EXT – SPACESTATION FAR SPACE 3, AN ANGULAR, IMPOSING STRUCTURE OF THREE CONCENTRIC TRIANGLES SET AGAINST A MAJESTIC STARSCAPE, SHIPS DOCKED WITH IT, SHUTTLES DEPARTING IT, PULSATING INTERDIMENSIONAL RIFT JUST BEYOND

INT – COMMAND DECK / 0800

Z-rank Sela Jar'i adjusted the shawl draped over her shoulders as she rode the lift up to the command deck. The white fabric covered her feathers down to mid torso and stood in contrast to her blue and green plumage. It was traditional for her species, and she wore it proudly to denote her rank on the station. *Z-rank* was a nickname she earned in the Strikers, and the ESC honored it by allowing her to keep it now.

The short ascent ended, and the lift glided to a stop exactly level with the floor. The command deck was accessible only by this lift, presumably in case of a Telosen uprising so the tiny crew of Atlins would be protected. It only had three rooms, this one, where all the senior staff worked at their stations, and branching off it was a conference room and the commander's office.

Lieutenant Aaza Kas-sti sat at the science station, monitoring the nearby rift for vessels entering or leaving. The red-furred wolf wore a green uniform designating her rank and function within the Democratic Earth & Space Command Committed to Peace and Democracy. It was designed to be antistatic so people covered in fur would be unencumbered, and she seemed comfortable enough, though Sela never understood how anyone in the ESC could be comfortable wearing so much clothing.

A reptile with black scales and yellow circles around his eyes and mouth lay underneath one of the consoles, a tangled pile of wires and circuit boards on the floor around him. Ihara was in charge of software updates to this station. Despite advances in hyperspace technology cutting travel time between solar systems from years into hours, and applied quantum entanglement making possible instant communication between planets thousands of light years apart, and graviton plating allowing people to walk on space ships without need for rotation, nobody could design a computer system for which software updates did not make things run worse. He had just recently installed the update to the computer voice, switching it from an Atlin male to a human female, and it had somehow broken the waste recycling system for three days.

The doors to the commander's office slid open, and Adrian Blunt stepped out.

The wolf glanced to the side. "Commander on deck."

Sela was already standing at attention. "Z-rank Sela Jar'i reporting for duty, sir."

Commander Blunt looked up from the tablet computer in his hands and nodded. His species, the human race, was the founding species of the ESC, and it represented all of the human-controlled worlds. It was only in the last thirty years or so their territory had expanded far enough to be considered an empire equal to the Stozi or the

Grovians, though the ESC did not call itself an empire. Merely a joint venture of its colonies to spread the good news about democracy, even among societies that were getting along just fine without it.

"We're expecting a delegation from Telosen at thirteen hundred hours."

Sela prepared for the worst. "Government or church?"

The commander smiled. "Neither. I'm told it's more of a tourist group."

"You called it a delegation."

"Technically it counts as one. They're all veterans of the Strikers who received high honors from the new democratically-elected council."

"And you want me to give the tour?"

His smile spread to a warm grin. "They would be thrilled to have a fellow Striker leading the way."

"Sure, I can show them the padlocks that kept every Telosen in their quarters, unlocking only when their shifts ended to allow them to visit the shops and buy food, and only after they recited some corporate policy in just the right tone of voice. I can show them the furnace where they burned the uniforms to force us to buy new ones every single year."

"Exactly," Commander Blunt said, strolling up to her. "You know what happened here. You can make history real. There will be children in the group. See to it they never forget the people who suffered. Hopefully it will never happen again, and the people of Telose will embrace democracy in the wake of it all."

He handed her the tablet. Sela took it from him—her species' wings had long ago become useless for flight and had developed fingers for grasping. The screen displayed suggestions for routes, likely made by members of the Telose council. Sela was already thinking of the stories she could tell of this place.

She looked up at him. "I'll do my best, sir."

"Thank you, Z-rank. I know you will." He turned and addressed the room. "Status reports."

The red wolf at the science station spoke first. "Inter-dimensional rift has been pulsing at the usual rate. No sign of activity in the last twenty-six hours."

The black reptile spoke from under the console. "Most of the centralized padlocks are off the quarters. Holographic body scanners removed from all of them, priority as requested."

Sela smiled at his belly. Ihara was a Fißeri, one of the ESC's more recent converts to democracy. He was incubating a clutch of eggs. All members of his species did, fertilized or not, a leftover survival trait. In primitive times, when threatened they would lay this clutch in the hopes of appeasing whatever predator was chasing them, allowing them to get away while it stopped to eat an easy meal. Since he still had his clutch, he certainly must not be too agitated by all these mandatory updates being pushed to the station by ESC command.

Blunt answered him. "We're in no rush, and we're ahead of schedule. Keep up the good work."

Sela crossed out two of the routes and had already settled on a combination of the first three. She had stories in mind. Lots of stories. Some too painful to speak aloud.

The wolf's console beeped. "Sir, we're receiving a message from an Atalor freighter approaching from Telose. They're requesting permission to dock for resupply and R-and-R."

"Grant them twenty-six hour permission."

Tablet under one wing, Sela turned and stepped onto the lift. She pressed the button and descended down to the security corridor. At the door, she leaned forward and let it scan her retina. With a chime, it slid to the side, and she stepped out.

INT – INNER DIAMOND

Various vendors had set up shop here to support the people who toiled at this station. Thousands of Telosen locked in their quarters for days at a time, bodies being recorded by holographic scanners and then quantum-beamed to far corners of the galaxy. Sela had been among them. Faking a smile for hours and hours at a time. Computer systems had monitored her eyes while she was on the clock, ensuring she presented the proper mood during and between calls. Algorithms monitored her voice to ensure she was within proper range. Maintaining her appearance and voice took conscious effort, and this was on top of the actual work she had to do here. Failure meant being expelled to the surface, where farming awaited her. Farming or cleric duties.

Sela narrowed her eyes as she walked along the lower level, glancing at the shops and pondering all of these flashy outlets and independent storefronts once covered up an entire population of workers who had no choice but to be happy and perky and enthusiastic. Sela's species expressed emotion with the eyes, and she had still not disassociated curling of the lips from Atlin oppression, so meeting humans had been especially difficult for her. She still winced just seeing Commander Blunt or Doctor Dorset smile.

Every day she served on this station reminded her of what had happened here, the suffering her people had endured for a century, and the effort the neighboring empires had made to help them rebuild, the human empire especially, seeing an opportunity to convert a weakened culture to democracy, the solution to every single problem in the universe.

The Atlins had built support stations just like this place all around her planet for generations. Entire cities of avians, now living on the surface, would likely not recover from the mental trauma of what they had to do here for decades, even with aid. FarS3 was the only such facility that had not been destroyed in the rebellion, and now it was being converted into a habitable space for the human empire as a jumping off point to continue to spread their political gospel.

The med-lab was just across the hall from Hadron's bar. Sela spared a glance at the nearly-naked Telsoe pouring drinks. He was wearing anti-gravity body rings this week, one encircling his waist, another encircling his chest, each barely covering him, and only from certain angles. Sela herself had tired to inform him this was fetish-wear for the Jakozi species, but he insisted fashion should have no connotations, and being fashionable was important to customer experience.

Hadron's establishment had been here since the Atlins first opened up the station. The avian was a master at disarming conversation and putting customers at ease. He was so good he actually did move up the ranks and was allowed to graduate from holographic representative to open an establishment of his own. The bar was busy, even this early in the workday, Hadron keeping it open at all times to cater to nocturnal species.

She squinted thinking that he was the only Telosen to have taken his employee training to heart. Sela considered him a traitor to the cause and to his species, but he stocked outstanding wine, and his wardrobe was entertaining, so she tolerated him.

Sela climbed the stairs to the second level and observed the people coming and going while she pondered the horror stories she could relate to the tour group. It was so hard to believe that only a year ago, this station had been full of slave laborers in finely-tailored uniforms.

As a member of the Strikers, Sela had helped thousands of people organize against this system of oppression. Their primary weapon was the sit-down strike. It created awkward situations that were broadcast across half the galaxy, and it got attention. After a century of oppression, facing stern condemnation from outside and the threat of unionization from the inside, the Atlins abandoned Telose, and thus began the slow healing process, and the equally slow process of converting this place into a space station fit for spreading the good news of human democracy. It was their only contribution to the galaxy, so most species humored them, as it gave the bald primates a sense of importance.

The lift from the crossway descended. Sela leaned on the rail and observed. Moments later, a crowded lift ascended. It was full of rough-skinned reptiles from Atalor.

One person stood out. A feline. Bipedal. Furless. Bones puckering the skin into raised ridges all around the head and neck and arms. Two of the Atalors were helping him walk. A human wearing an ESC uniform was leading them to the med-lab.

Sela's eyes widened.

The Atalors migrated out across the inner diamond, and the various shopkeepers tried to get their attention. Many went straight to Hadron's bar. The two reptiles led the gasping feline to the med-lab.

Sela's eyes narrowed, her kind's equivalent of a frown. She ran down the steps and crossed the corridor, stopping at the window looking into the med-lab. The feline was sitting on an exam bed, Doctor Dorset scanning him with a medical probe.

INT – MEDICAL LAB

She pushed the button on the panel, and the door slid to the side. Sela approached, stopping just two meters from the bed, out of the doctor's way. She and the feline locked eyes.

The human doctor turned around and met Sela's eyes. Doctor Lawrence Dorset was heterosexual and caucasian and comfortable with the gender assigned to him at birth. It was important to remember these facts, as they were easy to overlook. "Z-rank?" he said.

Sela touched the badge on the left side of her shawl. "Security to the med-lab. We have a Manager."

Doctor Dorset turned to his patient, and then back to Z-rank Jar'i. "What's going on?"

The Atlin coughed. "Forgive her, doctor. I'm sure it's just a reflex. Telosen tend to have this reaction to seeing Atlins again. She'll calm down once I leave."

Her eyes narrowed to slits. "Don't let this man out of your sight, doctor. He was my supervisor."

The feline on the exam table laughed. "What? Is being an Atlin a crime now?" His voice sounded gravely and hoarse.

The door behind her opened, and in flowed Cylinder, a living mass of transparent liquid. Cylinder frequently chose not to take a recognizable form, and today it maintained the shape of a tube of water wearing a Telosen shawl to denote its association with the nearby planet rather than the ESC. Two members of the security team flanked it, both Telosen, both carrying energy pistols aimed upward.

"Z-rank, what's the matter?" Cylinder asked, voice coming from its entire body. It rarely used a mouth to speak, and it somehow managed to keep its voice the same no matter what form it assumed.

"This Atlin is Mishi Hagan, and he was my supervisor on Far Space 3 for fifteen years. He deserves to stand before all of Telose and answer for what he did."

"Charmed... How can he help us?"

"Paul, we have an unusual request for you."

The mammal-lizard wagged his fluffy tail. "I like unusual requests."

His voice sounded dreamy. Sela wondered if he was using illicit substances.

"We need your help identifying this Atlin. He claims to be someone who once visited your establishment years ago. His scent profile matches, but his DNA profile only partially matches. It's a little confusing. We haven't been able to confirm his identity one way or another. We were about to conduct a lengthy, intricate investigation that would likely have involved twists and turns and political intrigue, but I suggested you might be able to save us the trouble."

Paul approached, his oversized equipment shaking and bouncing every step. His legs were digitigrade, like a canine, and yet he looked like a lizard from the front. His muzzle was long and pointed like canine but covered in scales. His ears were triangular, like a canine's, covered in fur. He moved more like a theropod than a canine. Rather birdlike, Sela thought.

Sela looked at their detainee. He was sweating. She partially winked one eye, the Telose gesture for a smile.

Paul approached, arms folded in front of his chest. He stood before of Patal and scented him. "Hmmm, he smells familiar." He leaned down to his stomach. "Yes, I recognize the scent. " He circled Patal, scenting his neck, then down his back and ending at the rear. He straightened up and flowed around to Patal's front side, snout to face with him.

Patal steeled himself in the face of the scaled canine. "My name is—"

Cylinder nudged him. "Paul will tell us your name."

Patal ignored him. "Scent profile already confirmed my identity, and my vocal damage is easily explained by the numerous lectures I've given over a long career. What else do you need?"

Z-rank Sela's feathers rose. "You can start by taking responsibility for the suffering you caused."

Patal grumbled and faced the shopkeeper. "Whatever you need to do to confirm my identity, do it."

Paul flicked his tongue across Patal's nose. He had a forked tongue in the shape of a canine's. "Undo your pants."

Patal's muzzle curled into a smile. Sela's smile dropped and now her eyes were wide. To her surprise, Patal was doing it. At first she turned away, but then she heard Paul moving, and she had to look.

The mammal-lizard was sucking the furless feline, eyes closed. Patal seemed to have forgotten where he was and was enjoying the moment. She looked at Cylinder. She saw its shape waver just a little, as if trying to mimic Paul's form, but each time it seemed to realize this and remained a formless fluid under a shawl.

She turned back to Paul and their detainee. Ignoring what he was doing, Sela could tell he was not merely sucking Patal.

"This is pointless," said the Atlin, panting through his nose. "My name is Patal K'eth. I already told you I am but a humble professor on Atlina Prime."

Sela narrowed her eyes at him. "You were a supervisor on Far Space 3. In fact, you were *my* supervisor."

Patal laughed, also trying not to look down at the lizard-mammal working his organ. "Is that what this is about? Vengeance against your boss?"

"Grievances, Mr. K'eth. Grievances. I would call customer service, but that's gone now, or did you set up shop somewhere else?"

"I was... *mmph*... aware of what was happening, but I have never served aboard a station."

"It's what the Atlins do. They landed and they promised us technology. We'd all have money and be able to participate in the economy beyond our planet. And what did you people do? You built Customer Support Stations! If a customer at one of your boutique stores had any grievance, they'd yell at us, not one of your own people."

"A mere matter of image, Z-rank. The Atlin empire prides itself on being the foremost producer and vendor of luxury clothing and electronics in the galaxy. Think what would have happened had we had to deal with our own technical issues?"

"And return desk complaints. It still hurts to think about. Have you ever worked customer service before, Mr. K'eth?"

He smiled. "Such work is beneath an Atlin. But is this really... a good time to pick open... old wounds?"

The scaled mammal opened his mouth and released him. He rose to meet the Atlin's eyes.

"Why did you do this yourself?"

Patal was still panting through his nose.

Cylinder extended itself and bound Patal's wrists. "Can you tell us who he is?"

"Wait here, please."

Paul turned and walked to a door at the rear of the room. He disappeared through it, leaving Sela and Cylinder to stare at Patal's throbbing erection.

Sela had never seen an Atlin's penis before. It was thin and pointed and had four fleshy barbs, one at each compass point. They looked like pieces of rounded bone poking out. He stood at full mast, patiently waiting for Paul to return.

The Atlin shook his head. "I won't wait for this shopkeeper. You caught me, Z-rank. I remember you. You were a good representative until the Strikers started filling your head with propaganda."

The avian was beak to nose with him. "Atlins never want to deal with their own problems! You used us! The entire galaxy hated us because we had to be the face of your problems! Your return policies! Your defective electronics!"

"Exactly the point.." He held her stare. "Telosen... A primitive species nobody had ever heard of. Not even space-faring when we arrived. What better way to introduce you to the entire galaxy than as the faces of our luxurious products?"

"Say it, Mishi! This is what your empire does! You told us you would bring us into society, but you wanted us to take the heat for your bad decisions!"

"That is propaganda and you know it. We gave you employment. I've read that when we arrived here, you were still in the bronze age. We taught you how to work. We raised you up, Z-rank. You learned about technology because of us."

Sela was pushing him backwards with her beak. "I was projected to the return desks of hundreds of your shops! Every time a customer wanted to complain about your shoes, or wanted to exchange something, I had to be the one to tell them we couldn't! Do you know how hard it is to maintain a happy voice and a bright pair of eyes telling someone it can't be done, knowing full well it can be!?"

"It could have been worse. You could have been working in a factory. It was ungrateful representatives like you that brought the whole system down."

"It will take Telosen generations to recover from the trauma you forced onto us! You. Mishi Hagan. You were the one that kept overriding me. Every single time I followed policy and refused a return, the customer would go over my head, and you would just let it through. We became the villains! Our entire species is infamous because of you! When we fought back, you called us terrorists. You tried to convince the entire universe *we* were unreasonable and horrible at interpersonal relations, but we showed them the truth, and now they know better!"

She noticed humming sounds coming from the rear door, along with the smell of polymer.

"You're a young woman." The Atlin held his ground, never breaking eye contact. "I don't expect you to remember this is the exact same debate we had for thirty years. I heard it over and over. We were doing you a favor, bringing you out of your farms and churches and into the field of customer service. There is no higher calling."

"I argued with an Atlin over a three-point price difference on a pair of gloves for two hours! Two hours I had to keep happy eyes and a cheerful voice or the computer would tell you I was inadequate!"

"I don't recall such a flagging, so you must have done well."

"Millions of my people suffered this indignity every single day for a hundred years! You made my life a living hell! If I'd had a gun, I would have shot you in the med-lab when I saw you!"

"Excellent customer service skills on display there, Z-rank."

"We fought back, and we won! The humans are helping us join the galaxy properly. It will take years to repair our image."

Now he narrowed his eyes at her, mimicking her facial expression. "How long have you been saving this anger, Z-rank? Nobody to call to voice your concerns. Nobody who cares. But now you found me. Does it feel nice to talk to a real person about your troubles? A real person who isn't reciting a rehearsed script."

Paul emerged, the door sliding shut behind him. He was holding two rolled-up discs of a polymer substance.

The reptilian canine paused, looking at each of them in turn, standing birdlike with his arms folded in front of him.

"You confused me at first," he began. "The scent is one person. The profile is another. Both of them visited my shop years ago." He held one of the polymer discs up. "Mishi Hagan." He raised the other one. "Patal K'eth."

The Atlin was sweating, but he had not gone soft.

Sela nodded. "Do it."

Paul approached the detainee and knelt. He placed the disc over the tip. Sela noticed the glowing blue line on the disc. The reptilian mammal was lining it up with the top center. He then rolled it down to the base.

Paul dropped his hands and observed. "I thought so. Hagan's was smaller, and the spurs don't match."

Sela and Cylinder both leaned over and observed. Not only were there bulges of extra polymer where spurs should have been, but they were not even the correct shape.

Paul peeled it off and set it on the floor. He then positioned the second disc over the tip. It was seeping liquid. Paul leaned over and licked it off before applying the disc. It practically unrolled itself, each spur finding a perfect home underneath a conformed bulge in the polymer, not a wrinkle anywhere on the shaft.

Paul looked up at him. "Patal K'eth, you changed your scent and your face, but you didn't change this. Why would you want everyone to think you're Mishi Hagan?"

Cylinder began flowing toward the door, pulling the Atlin. "Thank you, Paul. Come with us, please."

"Wait, wait!" Paul said, running after them, heavy sheath and gonads bouncing. He knelt in front of Patal, nuzzling his crotch. "I haven't had an Atlin in me in so long. Even Riack hasn't been here since the Atlins left."

Riack was the only Atlin aboard the station, operating a shop on the inner diamond that made jewel-encrusted eggs. Rumor had it he was of such low rank in their society that he had done customer service work. He was also a heterosexual, but not nearly on the same level as Doctor Dorset.

"We don't have time for this," Sela said.

Paul waved his tail about. "In my shop, my client decides what he wants to do once he has one of my sleeves on, and he *is* a paying client."

Sela narrowed her eyes and looked at the Fluidic. The water was difficult to read, but its moods often came through in whatever waves and vibrations and physical shapes it assumed. Right now tiny ripples bounced around inside it. Cylinder was amused. It relaxed its liquid grip on Patal and retracted fully into itself, standing as a wall of water under an avian shawl. Sela couldn't believe it was yielding to this creature, and to her surprise, Patal stepped forward and nudged the lizard-fox onto his back. He shoved himself in with very little effort, and without any kind of obvious lubricant, Sela noticed. Paul sprawled out.

"Oooooohaah, I always enjoy those spurs."

Patal lay on top of Paul, holding his arms on the floor. Now all his fur was hidden, and all Sela and Cylinder could see was the scaled underside.

Sela looked at Cylinder, wondering if they should do something. Cylinder had no eyes or face most of the time, so she could never tell which way it was looking.

Patal was not gentle, and now he was using his knees to pin Paul's legs to the floor. The hybrid was splayed as wide as he could be, and Patal was going deep and fast, pulling all the way out and then shoving all the way back in.

Sela pretended to look around as well, but she couldn't take her eyes away. How could she have been here all this time and not known this shop existed? Why had nobody mentioned it?

Paul's throbbing erection peeked out from under the Atlin. It dwarfed anything Sela had seen before, and she wondered why such a small creature had such enormous parts. It had changed to a greenish color and it was leaking all over his scales as Patal pushed in to the hilt, and then tried to go in even deeper. Paul lay there, eyes closed, moaning and shuddering.

One last move, then a thrust even deeper, and the Atlin held still, lying snout to snout with Paul. The hybrid rubbed muzzles with him, and Patal's grip relaxed.

Patal pulled out, polymer sleeve ballooned with seed. He rolled over, completely spent. Paul unsprawled himself and panted, tail beating the floor.

"Mishi Hagan," Patal began, looking over at the living tube of water and Z-rank Sela. "He needs to answer for what he did. Do you have any idea what it was like in that room? I was told to make customers happy, knowing the whole time I was throwing you and everyone else under the bus, but Hagan told us to give the customer what they wanted simply because he didn't want to deal with them! My people should be the ones the universe hates, not yours! Everyone needs to know what *we* did! I was a manager but I couldn't do anything. Atlina Prime will just find a new planet to set up call centers. A new planet full of primitive people to use as the face of their problems just to save their own reputation—because *we* don't want to handle any of it ourselves!"

Sela knelt beside Patal as he peeled off the polymer sleeve. He dropped the little bag of grey seed on the floor beside him. Paul had not moved. He was spent, and yet he had not finished.

"It wasn't your fault," Sela said.

He reached out and held her by the shoulder. "Let me be the face of what my people did to yours. What you did just now—the rage you expressed—an entire species is suffering from pent up anger about their time in customer service. I can be the object of that hatred. Hagan needs to be that object. I can give your people the relief they need. It will force Atlina Prime to deal with its own problems for once. It has to."

"Maybe there's a way," Sela said, helping Patal to his feet. He was pulling his pants up. "Someone will see through it."

"Please forgive me! Please forgive us! I couldn't even tell my children what I thought about this—they would have reported me to the police! I'm so sorry!"

"Come on. I'll buy you a drink at Hadron's."

Now decent again, Sela and Cylinder led him to the door. Cylinder did not have to bind his hands anymore. Sela remained behind as the other two walked out. She turned to Paul.

"Thanks for your help."

"Any time." Dreamy voice again.

"You probably saved us a lot of time. I wanted to believe that man was Mishi Hagan. I'm honestly a little impressed you met him."

"His cock was smaller, but he placed larger orders."

"That's... hardly important. Do you even know who Mishi Hagan was?"

The creature licked his lips. Sela continued.

"He was my supervisor on FarS3 when it was a call center. One of hundreds of stations surrounding my planet. Mishi Hagan told us to follow the rules and enforce policy, but then he would override us every time a customer complaint made it up to his level. It's because of him the Telosen rose up against the Customer Support Stations and..."

Sela would have continued rattling off the numerous atrocities Mishi Hagan was guilty of, but the creature yawned and scratched his muzzle with his hind paw. She looked over his mismatched scales and fur and the ridiculous proportions of his male parts. She smiled with her eyes. "What exactly are you?"

"I'm Paul." He panted, tongue hanging out. "I'm a Construct."

"Never met one before. Where does your kind come from?"

"I'm not sure, but I think it was a long ways from here."

"I see. What's your real name?"

"Paul is my name. It's what the Atlins called me when they ran the station. It sounds like their word for vagina."

"That's definitely something they would do. And... what does CCS stand for?"

"Custom Contraceptive Shop, the most comfortable in the solar system."

Sela partially winked one eye. "Next time I hook up with someone, I'm bringing him here. With all the people coming through the rift, who knows what they're bringing with them."

Paul tilted his head. "Rift?"

"Yes, the interdimensional rift in spacetime."

He turned to her, mouth open, tongue hanging out and touching the carpet.

"You haven't heard? It's been open for months."

He did not react.

Sela's feathers flared and settled. "It leads to a another universe, possibly another plane of existence. Doesn't seem to be any liquid water over there. We've already made contact with a dozen new species from the other side, and none of their bodies use water the way ours do. It's a fascinating place."

He continued looking at her dreamily.

She went on. "Ihara helped someone escape predators."

"He did?"

"She told us her species produces its own water. They never need to drink. A predator race hunts them; her species is their only source of water. It ended in a laser battle that triggered a station-wide alert. Ihara even lost his clutch. It happened right outside your shop. You can't tell me you didn't hear."

He curled up and sighed. "I've been in here. I only know what people tell me."

She stared at him for a moment. "You should probably ask your clients to keep you informed. A lot's happened on this station since the ESC took command of it."

Paul rolled to his side, facing her, chessboard sheath and testicles squished between his legs. "Doesn't really matter to me."

"Well, I promise to send anyone I meet your way."

He was panting heavily, oversized junk jiggling. "Please do. I love taking new clients."

She partially winked the other eye and then followed the tube of water and the feline onto the inner diamond.

"There's a tour group coming, Mr. K'eth. Can I persuade you to say a few words? Maybe even accompany me as I lead it?"

Patal looked at her. He smiled. The gesture did not make Sela wince.

2

INT – PAUL'S SHOP / 1100

The Stozi's organ emerged from its sheath. The entire structure formed a long, rigid cone. Upon stimulation, smaller cones rose from the surface in a spiral pattern from tip to base. Paul's tongue told him that these fleshy barbs also lifted up and had patterns of barbs over them as well. The subtleties of each Stozi were a treat to explore, and a challenge to duplicate; if one barb was not aligned correctly, the entire sleeve would not fit.

Paul lay on his back under the quadruped, hands around his hind ankles, which were twice as thick as Paul's hands could grip.

Paul had been told that the Stozi had deeply ingrained reactions to facial expressions and tail movements. Even the slightest twitch of a muscle on the muzzle, or a flick of the tail, triggered powerful instinctive responses, and it had kept them locked in a rigid social structure for generations, individuals and groups learning complex rituals of etiquette to avoid arousing a reaction in someone else. For the sake of freeing their minds, they cut off their children's muzzles and tails at birth, depriving them of their usual means of expressing emotion. By extension, they also disciplined themselves to celibacy, mating only during their annual cycle.

That's what they told people.

Paul had made custom sleeves for so many Stozi over the years he was convinced nobody actually followed that directive—that the entire species, in fact, experienced the full range of emotions but lacked the ability to express them, so they were all trapped inside themselves, and sex was the only outlet they had. He once overheard Hadron say that the Stozi may no longer be tossed about by impulsive reactions to the body language of others, freeing them to focus on mathematics and the arts and invent space travel and so forth, but that did not mean everyone was content.

Paul had this quadruped's entire organ mapped in his mind, and he released the client and slid out from under him.

"Wait here if you wish. I will have a proof ready shortly."

The Stozi spoke evenly, lacking inflection. "Thank you."

Paul turned to the beds. Two Telosen sat on one of the beds, both of them hard, and a human sat on the other, pants around his ankles and flaccid. Paul noticed he bore the rank of ensign, and the other two ESC officers flanking him were fully clothed. They had brought him here as a hazing ritual, probably. Paul did not care so long as they followed the rules and someone ended up inside him.

Paul wagged his tail and moved to the Telose bed. The two birds winked their eyes, smiling at him, leaning backwards. Paul began with the one on the left, dropping to his knees and opening his mouth. He closed his eyes and took the entire thing in one motion.

Telosen had multi-pronged members, which made effective contraceptives for them difficult to make. The number of stalks each bird had varied between individuals, but at least those stalks were smooth. Each one could move individually, designed to stimulate the interior of a person as needed. The most interesting part was how a male from Telose had control of each stalk. They could explore the interior as if with fingers. This male had five stalks emerging from his slit, each about the size of Paul's finger, each one moving around inside his mouth and ending at a point. He liked how the Telosen teased his insides, feeling him all around until they found exactly where Paul liked it.

Having analyzed this male's most sensitive parts, Paul rose and crouched in front of the second person on the bed. He opened his mouth and swallowed the wiggling tendrils. This male had three stalks, but proportionally thicker to compensate. They twisted around one another inside Paul's muzzle. Paul analyzed every square centimeter of him, and then released him.

"I have both of your profiles," Paul said as he rose to his hind paws. "I will have proofs ready shortly."

They were both winking and squinting. The one on the left spoke. "So which one did you like better?"

Paul wagged his tail. "I liked the complexity of your stalks. It's like a maze for my tongue to work through. But," he looked at the male on the right, who had fewer but thicker stalks wiggling from his slit, "I also liked how he keeps his twisted up. It's like a puzzle for me to work to separate them."

"He likes doing that," the left bird said. "He only unwraps them after fucking me for a while."

The right-hand bird pecked the left bird with his beak. "I make you earn it."

Paul left them to peck and flap at one another and walked to the other bed and the nervous human.

"Hello, my name is Paul."

The two ESC officers standing on either side of him smiled. The one on the right spoke. "Our buddy Justin here needs what you're selling."

Paul's tail flicked to the side. "Everyone needs what I'm selling."

The left human smiled wider. "He just graduated from the academy and heard about all the venereal diseases out there, so now he's scared."

Paul knelt between his legs and looked up at him. "Yes, so many that can cross species lines. Just relax and I'll build you a profile. We only have to do this once. Are you ready?"

"S-sure."

Paul began licking. It did not take much stimulation to make the ensign hard. The human sex organ could curve up, down, to the side, or not at all. Sometimes it had bumps along the head, sometimes not. Some cultures cut off the skin covering the tip, others left it alone. Thickness and length varied quite a bit, but the basic structure was always the same. The ensign was unremarkable in terms of shape and size, but the skin folds fascinated Paul. After just a minute, he had his contours memorized. Paul let it slide out of his mouth and rose to his hind paws.

"That was fast," said the ensign.

"Humans are easy," Paul replied, and addressed the room. "A few moments please while I build your proofs."

Paul left everyone sitting around with their cocks fully engorged. He walked to the room in the back and then shut the door behind him.

Paul stood at the terminal and began typing. The computer had numerous algorithms he could use to speed up the data entry, and he used one of them now to duplicate the fractal patterns he had felt on the Stozi. All he had to do was enter the initial shape, and then tell the computer how to distribute smaller versions of that structure around the whole.

The two Telosen were more challenging, but he had already built basic algorithms to describe them. He only had to input the variations, and he typed them in so rapidly he occasionally outpaced the computer screen.

Paul remembered years ago an Eneg had set up a rival shop on the other side of the inner diamond. The Eneg had used a scanner and a computer to generate the profiles and build sleeves. Paul knew people who had tried both, and they kept coming back to Paul's shop. Paul's muzzle was more accurate than a scanner.

Plus, the Eneg had not provided free and immediate trials of his product.

Both Telosen sleeves made, Paul now moved on to the human. He entered the bézier curves and control points so fast he watched the penis take shape on the screen in real time. As he typed in the numbers describing the details, he watched the texture of the skin form on screen from bottom to top. He rotated the penis on screen, and his eyes told him he had entered all the numbers correctly.

He sent all four patterns to the polymer machine behind him. As it built the sleeves, Paul rubbed himself, anticipating how each one would feel inside him. He looked forward to the three-stalked Telose most. He imagined all three stalks going in as one and remaining rigid until the muscles relaxed and they started exploring him.

Paul slipped out of his sheath. His own organ was a blend of canine and reptile, pointed and pronged on either side, but ending with a knot. It had not inflated yet. Right now it was purple, and it would change color depending on how close he was to climax.

The printer ejected four rolled-up discs. Paul could tell whose was whose just by the circumference, and he arranged them from largest to smallest so they fit in a neat, pyramidal stack in his paw. He pushed the button. The door slid open. Everyone was sitting on or near the closest bed, checking one another out. Paul drew their attention, and he went to each one and slipped on the sleeve. As usual, the new clients marveled at how perfect it fit. So perfect it didn't shift at all.

Paul climbed up the bed between his clients and knelt on it, tail up. Apparently everyone had come to agreement regarding who would be first, as they led the nervous ESC officer behind Paul, and then he felt the human slip under his tail.

The human organ always made Paul feel relaxed and content. Something about the smoothness of the shaft and the way the skin moved over the tip inside him. He designed their sleeves to work with or without the skin over the tip, and now this ESC officer was starting to feel the appeal.

He was a slow and tender partner, and Paul lay flat on the bed, pulling him down with him. Now able to lie flat on Paul and feel his fur, he thrust faster. This was the part Paul liked best—when someone became so comfortable they would lead Paul around. The ensign gradually wrapped his arms around Paul's reptile chest and pulled him to his side. He was able to get much, much deeper with this angle, and as he lost himself in the motions, he became more confident.

Paul opened his eyes and noticed the others were rubbing themselves to stay hard. The two Telosen sometimes felt each other, twirling the stalks around their fingers, making each other gasp.

The human squeezed Paul so hard as he thrust Paul quickly ran out of breath to gasp or moan. The ensign finished and slowly released Paul. His fellow ESC officers slapped him on the shoulder and ushered him off the bed.

The Stozi went next. The quadruped climbed up on the bed and lay against Paul. The large mammal cocooned him between all four legs, and Paul felt his sleeved organ against his rear.

Quickly he felt the fractal pattern slide into him. The sleeve he had designed had minuscule pockets for every raised spine to reside, going three fractals deep. His tongue could sense even more miniature, raised cones rising from those, but the polymer had a limited resolution, and details that small did not make much of a difference.

The Stozi rolled Paul around so he lay on his back, and Paul lay belly up on the Stozi's stomach, four legs still wrapped around him. He bucked his hips so hard his testicles swung upward and smacked Paul's a few times. Paul held his forepaws and enjoyed being held in place.

The quadruped lowered his hind legs and used them to thrust deeper and faster. Paul now felt the hilt of the sleeve brushing him, and he knew he had mapped the cones properly.

Paul drifted into a dreamlike state for a moment as the Stozi found a pleasing rhythm, and then he was pulling out. The two Telosen were gesturing the Stozi to roll him around, and he rolled Paul off the side of the bed. Paul landed on his feet, panting and holding his hands together. One of the Telosen turned him around and bent him over the side of the bed. Paul couldn't raise his tail high enough.

He felt a trio of twisted stalks slide into him, and Paul moaned, happy to feel those stalks inside him, rigid and wonderful. It felt like a mammal's organ like this, an exotic sensation.

He felt counter-thrusts. He glanced over his shoulder to see the other Telose behind him, fucking the first one. They were preening one another's neck feathers as they shared this moment.

The harder he thrust, the more relaxed the stalks became. Paul lay halfway on the bed and pictured them in his mind, slowly untwisting and about to start teasing his insides.

As he thought it, Paul felt three little fingers feeling around in him, and he squirmed and pushed his hips back. This encouraged the avian to thrust harder. When his partner thrust him, he pushed into Paul. They kept this rhythm going for a while.

Paul felt all three stalks spreading out inside him. Paul's tongue hung from his mouth as they explored him, and then one last thrust.

When a Telosen pulled out, they were physically incapable of contracting their stalks, so each one spread Paul on the way. Paul gasped and nuzzled the bed as he did.

His partner still wasn't done with him, and he dropped to his knees while his five-stalked companion mounted him. Paul wagged his tail, disappointed not to feel five prongs inside him, but content with what he had. They ordered three boxes each, ten per box. Paul hoped one of them would remain behind and use him again while he ran off more copies, but they all left for Hadron's.

Paul went back to the printer. He set the boxes in a line and let the machine run off multiple copies of each profile. As he waited for the first profile to finish, he rubbed himself. His lizard-canine cock was still out of its sheath, now shaded pink. Still one more color to go before he reached climax. He was disappointed nobody had managed to stimulate him all way. He thought for sure one of the Telosen would be able to—one of their stalks would find the right spot and stay there, but they seemed to be actively avoiding those places inside him. He wondered if they were saving that for later, or if they were just inconsiderate. Paul sighed as he breathed the smell of hot polymer.

The first order was done. Paul set the boxes to the side and printed the second. He collected the rolled discs one by one and placed them in the box. His mind drifted to the Grovians, those bipedal dinosaur-creatures. Humans said they resembled T-rexes, but Paul was not sure what they meant by that.

The saurian species centered its entire society around war. Everything was about battle to them; even during times of peace they found a way to prove themselves through combat. The genders looked, sounded, and dressed identically. They performed identical roles in society. One only knew which gender a Grovian was when they took off their clothes and exposed themselves, rare between members of their own kind, and even rarer in the presence of alien races. They had special pronouns which had no translation among any species, thus they became the first words in Grovian others learned to speak.

When they took partners, they did not care if it would produce a child. Only that the union would benefit the status of both families. Paul had been privileged to know many of them intimately. He'd heard ESC officers say anyone who entered Paul's shop had to be male, but Paul had noticed many Grovians enter his shop simply to watch Paul work. It amused them to watch males take turns on Paul. A Grovian dick was ridged in the same way as their scales all the way down the shaft. Similar in basic structure to a human's, but thicker. He was in the mood to feel those ridges deep inside himself.

He turned to the computer and pulled up his favorite profile. Seeing the penis on the screen reminded him of the day he had met urm. He could see gres muzzle, gres white eyes, gres green, pebbly skin. Akaak, House of Ihi. He remembered how heavy gres body had felt lying on top of him, how those spongy ridges felt. Paul had made the sleeve precise enough to contour the ridges perfectly, and every single one of them brushed against his sensitive spots. Everything Akaak did had made Paul whine. Paul had never seen his dick change color so fast, and he had finished twice before Akaak had once, which had impressed the saurian.

He sent a command to the printer. Three copies. They printed after the second order.

Paul held them in his hand. It had been years since Akaak had been here. Not since the Atlins were still running this station.

He collected the last two orders and set them on the desk. He checked his messages. Five new requests from previous clients, all next-day orders. Paul sent the commands to the printer and lined the boxes up. While he waited, he unrolled one of the Akaak copies. It formed a perfect, hollow duplicate of what was in Akaak's slit. He felt the pointed tip that expanded thicker than Paul's hand grip, fleshy ridges lining it. He traced the contours with a finger, turning to the door several times.

One by one the four clients from earlier returned, and Paul had their orders ready. They smirked at his erection, and to Paul's disappointment they did not have the energy to go again or the time to help him finish. Climax was never required for Paul to enjoy it—just feeling someone inside him was quite enough to make him happy—but he did like to finish every now and then, even if the cleanup cost him money.

They also asked what the unrolled sleeve and the two rolled pieces on the chair were for, and Paul joked he was trying to summon a former client of his.

Four satisfied clients. Five returning clients coming tomorrow. He had made his money for the day, and he considered closing up and resting, but he decided to wait. Paul sat on one of the beds and watched the door, making sure his privates were easily visible to anyone entering.

INT – PAUL'S SHOP / 2500

No new clients for the rest of the day, but four more reprint orders came through. After running them off and boxing them up, Paul switched off the sign on the outside and climbed into the closest Telosen bed. The birds from Telose once built nests out of grass, so they made their beds to mimic the feeling of sleeping on grass. He curled up under the cover and imagined Akaak climbing into bed behind him and enveloping Paul in gres muscular grip. He raised a leg and imagined feeling those ridges.

The sounds from Hadron's bar began to wane. The ambient footsteps marching up and down the inner diamond gave way to the low hum of electricity flowing through the conduits overhead and below and through the walls. Paul felt the air moving about the room. The gentle breeze from the two air vents puffed his fur. He pulled the cover over himself, leaving only his muzzle exposed. From the room beyond, he heard another order drop into the queue. He was tempted to get up and fill the order now, but he was too comfortable.

He hoped he'd meet a Grovian client tomorrow. Grovians so rarely visited the station these days. Clients in general rarely mounted him after he had made their initial pattern, but Akaak had come back several times, and each time Paul had invited urm to stay after hours.

For a few weeks, Paul had let someone mount him without a sleeve, and he had felt those wonderful ridges moving inside him. Doctor Dorset, who was heterosexual no matter how many times he mounted Paul, had once told him the Grovians had an aggressive territorial drive as part of their mating instinct, which they had diverted into a warrior culture: flashy, posturing, always shouting. Paul knew when alone and in bed, they could be gentle and caring. Akaak was a slow and passionate partner. Je had taken a liking to Paul and spent the night with him multiple times —one of the few clients who actually asked about him personally.

Gres semen was so warm Paul felt the heat in his throat. Paul had told urm his penis changed color to black when he was about to finish, and Akaak had wrapped gres muzzle around Paul's length and swallowed it, all the while still moving back and forth inside him. When he woke up, Akaak was still there, arms still wrapped around him, and Paul had never felt better.

He had offered Akaak to take gres boxes free of charge, but the Grovian had insisted on paying full price every time. They had spent many nights together before gres ship undocked from the station. It had felt so good to be with someone instead of just doing business all day.

So many years ago.

Paul heard a strange noise coming from the vent. He opened his eyes and threw off the cover. It sounded like liquid flowing through the air vent. Paul stood on the bed and followed it from the wall. The sound moved with the duct. Paul rose to full height and loosened the vent cover over his head.

The liquid sound was coming closer. Paul jumped and grabbed the edge. He pulled himself up just high enough to see inside the vent. His night vision cut through the darkness, and now he saw a mass of liquid coming straight for him. The flow slammed into him, but instead of flowing around him, it wrapped around his head. Paul couldn't even open his mouth—it was exerting force. He slipped out of the vent and fell to the bed, landing on his back, the writhing mass flowing over and around him.

Finally it washed over him and flowed onto the bed. Paul sat up, tail raised. The clear ooze flowed all over the bed, as if searching for a way out. Finally Paul breathed.

"Cylinder?"

The liquid did not react.

Paul leaned forward. "Cylinder, are you sleepwalking again?"

The ooze settled at the foot of the bed and stretched upwards. A form began to emerge. Feathers. Beak. Arms. Legs. But it was still undulating like a liquid, and the feathers were not separate, rather they formed a single sheet that hung off the torso. It also stood twice as tall as a typical Telose bird. A transparent Telosen now loomed on the bed. Cylinder barely seemed able to hold this shape, as the bird form was wilting.

It reached for Paul, arm stretching and becoming thinner. It moaned. The moan stretched along with the arm, becoming a high-pitched roar.

At first Paul wanted to cuddle up to the liquid and let it flow over and through him, but the arm pushed Paul off the bed. He backed up, hands folded in front of him. Cylinder's other arm now stretched in his direction, still groaning and roaring.

"Cylinder, wake up."

Paul had seen it sleepwalk before, but never like this. Normally all he had to do was caress the puddle and Cylinder would eventually settle. This time Cylinder wasn't just having a nightmare; it had become the nightmare.

The melting facsimile of a Telose bird must have reached its limit, and now it flowed off the bed and stood on the carpet, growing new limbs and flailing them about. When it touched the carpet, a ripple ran through its body. The sheet of feathers receded into its liquid body. So did the beak. Now a feline form emerged from the ooze. The Atlin body before Paul was featureless, only the most broad traits and form of the species. It lumbered toward Paul on barely-formed legs, flowing as if the carpet were ice and this Atlin's legs had been severed at the thighs.

Paul backed up to the chair and stood behind it, not wanting to be shoved again. The shrieking, melting Atlin slid toward him.

It was just a couple meters from the chair, now losing its Atlin shape and melting into a blob with stumpy limbs.

"Did something bad happen?"

It reached the chair and began to flow over it. As it moved over the backrest, the melting liquid tightened into a vaguely saurian shape. In a few seconds, the form settled into pebbly skin. Blunt, curved muzzle. Not just a featureless reptile from Grovi. It was Akaak's body, exactly as it had been, rendered in water.

Paul rose from behind the chair, looking the creature over. Cylinder was wearing the unrolled sleeve Paul had left on the chair.

The creature was still shrieking. Paul gritted his teeth and lunged for him, embracing his torso. He cried and held him tight, muzzle buried in his chest. The body was not completely solid. It seemed to be threatening to melt and collapse on top of him any moment, but Paul held it and cried.

Cylinder held still. It wasn't reaching or moaning anymore. Now Paul felt a large hand on his back, five claws running through his fur. A low-pitched growl resonated from the body. It rose to a shriek. It solidified.

It was still angry.

Paul turned around and raised his tail. Instantly he felt the half-liquid body flowing on top of him. The only solid part seemed to be whatever was contained inside the sleeve. Special glands inside Paul produced a lubricant, and it slid in with little resistance.

The liquid mass could not hold the shape, but it still loomed over Paul, halfway between a formless liquid and a Grovian.

It did not thrust, but the organ matched exactly, and for a moment Paul let himself believe Akaak had returned. Je never had to thrust. Just lying together had been more than enough.

Paul's arms gave out, and he fell to the carpet, body squeezed under the weight of this liquid. Paul mumbled as the solid organ moved in him. The contrast between the fluid pushing his body down and the hard organ deep inside him made him slip into that dream state he craved so much.

When he opened his eyes again, he was under a dome of fluid. It touched every hair and scale on his body. It even massaged his eyes and filled his ears. Paul had no senses now.

And yet the organ inside him remained solid. The ridges were so perfect Paul still imagined Akaak on top of him, using gres mass to pin him down but still being so tender and gentle.

When he became aware again, the weight lifted off Paul's back. The dense fluid receded from his eyes and released his head. The pressure under his tail eased as it slipped out. Paul rolled over and faced Cylinder. Its liquid body was beginning to settle into the Grovian form, curled into fetal position.

Having now taken on a saurian form, it stared at Paul. Cylinder's features were vague enough to see Akaak lying in front of him. Paul crawled to urm and curled up. He knew this was not Akaak, but he couldn't stop the emotional rush. At first Cylinder remained rigid and uncertain about what it was supposed to do, and then it simply rested an arm over Paul and lay with him, hip to hip, muzzle to muzzle.

INT – PAUL'S SHOP / 0918

The door chimed. Paul peeked from his sheath at the thought of a new client so early in the day. He pushed the button behind the desk and unlocked the door. A wall of water wearing a shawl walked in, tablet suspended inside its body about where the waist would be on a bipedal creature. It hesitated and then began vibrating in a vocal range.

"Good... Good morning, Paul."

"Cylinder," Paul said, rising from his seat, still peaking from his sheath. "Is something wrong?"

"I, uh, wanted to follow up regarding our encounter last night."

Paul walked around the desk and embraced Cylinder. The Fluidic stood stiffly, barely a ripple. It had solidified its body enough to prevent Paul from falling into it.

"I knew it was you, but it was so nice to feel a Grovian in me again. Akaak. It was just like urm. I wanted to be with urm again so much. It was a wonderful night. Thank you for being with me."

"I owe you gratitude for helping me last night as well," Cylinder said.

Paul released it and moved to the bed. He sat, making a nest for his male parts to rest in. "You were sleepwalking and screaming."

"I was furious."

"What happened?"

"You really do need to get out more. So much is happening on this station even I can't keep up. Doctor Resho was here."

"I think I remember. You mentioned him once, when the Atlins were running the station. You said he was your father."

Cylinder nodded. "He is, in a sense. He discovered me in a filter on a dye-making plant on a human planet several hundred light years from here. To the scientists, I was a globule of dense water. He tried to find... *uses* for me. He came to the station the other day. I believe I was on my way to the med-lab the other night when I ran into you. I was in something between sleep and awake. I would have harmed him if you hadn't kept me occupied."

Paul tilted his head. "Why would you do that?"

"He quit his lab work and devoted all his time to trying to find some industrial application for me. Under a microscope, I am just water molecules, impurities from the ocean and all. Scientifically, I am not alive, so he tried to use me to filter chemicals from air, water, toxins from the body. He exposed me to all sorts of substances. One day, I was able to reach out to him and tell him I wasn't just some strange new type of water. Even knowing I was alive and showed signs of intelligence, he still put me inside of factory equipment to clean it out or separate isotopes. That's where I stayed for months at a time. Filtering dye at factories. Filtering gold from slurry at mines. He traveled around ESC, Eneg, and Atlin territory, offering me as a freelance solution to uncommon problems their machines had. He even forced me into the bodies of some Telose workers to find out if I could keep them hydrated all day without needing to provide water to their workers. The Atlins were always searching for ways to keep their public face on stage longer.

"He rebuked me every time I tried to show myself as an intelligent person. I had to do all of that in secret, on my off days, so to speak. He helped me learn language and how to imitate the proper forms and voices. Resho and I had a long talk this morning. For the first time in my life, I told him what I thought of him. I hated that he taught me to imitate his voice. To mimic clothes. To imitate his body. He insisted I always be opaque, with a male voice, and have two legs. He said it was proper appearance, but I hated how he kept trying to make me into his own image. Most of all, I hated the work he made me do. It turns out I was his only source of income. That's what he trying to protect. He wasn't thinking of me, and he regrets it now. It took him all these years to find me. He came back to ask for forgiveness, and if we could start over. Maybe even make up for what he put me through."

"I grew up in a lab, too," Paul said, ears dropping. "But... I miss it."

Cylinder approached the bed. "Thank you for your help, Paul. If you hadn't held me back, I don't want to think about what I would have done to Doctor Resho. I never let myself feel resentment toward the man. I wasn't even aware I had such strong feelings about my youth. About him."

Paul raised his head, hoping Cylinder would touch him. "I'm happy I could help."

The tablet inside Cylinder's body flowed toward Paul, partially sticking out from its torso. "I wanted to give you this as a thank-you, but I'm afraid it's probably not what you really wanted to know."

Paul took the handheld computer. It wasn't wet, and Paul thought it was strange that Cylinder never left any water behind. He recognized the Grovian language on the left column and an automated translation on the right. It displayed a familiar face.

"You called the name Akaak several times the other night. I became curious about the form I assumed and contacted the Grovian archives. Perhaps it will give you some closure."

Paul looked up. He could read a little, but most of the words made no sense to him, even when he recognized them.

"Akaak, House of Ihi, was fourth officer on a patrol ship assigned to the Grovian border with Atlin territory. Je was killed five years ago in a skirmish with them."

Paul felt sick to his stomach. Cylinder leaned over and extended itself. It held his shoulder.

"Who was je?"

Paul stared at the image on the screen. "One of the only people who wanted to see me after hours. Je really did care about me. It wasn't just business."

"I'm very sorry, but if you scroll to the bottom, you'll find something interesting."

Paul touched the screen and moved the feed down to the bottom. The duel text columns scrolled simultaneously. He read, only catching a few words here and there. He recognized his name, the word for the sleeves he made, and an order request.

"I don't understand. Why are they ordering from me?"

"Grovians commemorate battles with a relic from the battlefield. Usually a claw or a tooth, but sometimes pieces of skin or the ship. Akaak was the last of gres line in the House. For gres House's honor to be restored, a relic from the battlefield needs to be returned. None was because Atlins vaporized the remains as a deliberate insult. I informed gres relatives about you, and they believe what you have qualifies as a relic of battle."

Paul's tail wagged.

3

INT – PAUL'S SHOP / 1300

Paul lay face down rear up on the bed. The human behind him was buried to the hilt, marveling at how perfect the sleeve fit and he didn't feel afraid it would slip off. Paul hoped he would keep this up for hours. He whimpered and wagged his tail as the human thrust.

Alas, just minutes later the human finished. He felt the fur on Paul's back and ran his hand around to Paul's underside to feel his scales. Paul held his hand. He pulled out, and just as Paul took a breath, he felt someone else climbing up behind him. Another sleeved organ slid into him. Another human. Paul was still getting a lot of them.

The first was depositing the used sleeve in the can by the door as he pulled up his pants. "That was amazing. Sign me up for few boxes of those."

Paul moaned while he spoke. "Send me an order request. I can have them ready in an hour. Small discount for next-day orders."

"Do you deliver?"

"Mmm—mmm—aaah—mmmmaahhh—depends if any freighters are going your way. They'll charge a fee, too."

"I'll keep that in mind. Thanks." He turned and walked out the door.

"Good day—ooooh."

The human was speeding up. Paul held his hand as the human felt his stomach and chest.

"Damn, I'm almost there! Never finished this fast before!"

"It's—ah—what happens—ah-ah—when you have—haaaahaaaa—a sleeve that fits."

The human grabbed Paul's furry ears and pounded him deep and fast. Gradually one hand wandered down to his scaly sheath. He felt it all around, as well as his testicles.

"These things are huge." He then felt Paul's length. "Wow. I think you put everyone on the station to shame."

Paul was lost in the feeling of being full. The human slammed him harder and harder a few more times, and then stopped. Moments later, he pulled out, and another ESC human stepped in behind him and began thrusting.

The previous human pulled the sleeve off and dropped it in the can. He walked back to the bed as he re-did his pants. He held Paul's muzzle as the third ESC recruit began.

"What species are you?" he asked.

Paul opened one eye and panted through his nose. "Ahh... Mmmmmm... Ahhhh."

"I've never seen anyone like you before. Front half lizard, back half canine, color-changing dick. What planet are you from?"

"Mmm—ahhhh—mmmm—doesn't matter."

"Has that very heterosexual and caucasian doctor ever done a DNA profile on you?"

"Doctor Dorset checks on me—aaahhhhhh—once in a while."

"Everyone keeps telling me you don't have quarters. Is that true?"

"I live here." The human behind him had found a pleasing rhythm.

"And you never leave?"

"No reason to."

"Come to my quarters if you like. Or we'll share a drink at Hadron's."

"I'm happy here."

"Offer's open. Right, Mitch?"

The human had found a faster rhythm. "Yes, yes, *yes!*"

The other human climbed on the bed and held Paul's face. He scooted over, Paul raised himself up, and he rested his head in his lap as the other human quickened his pace. Paul panted. Moments later, the human pulled out, leaving Paul feeling empty and wishing someone else would step in and fill him up again, all day, no end.

He rolled halfway over and lay on the bed, panting. Both humans stood up and held one another around the waist.

"I like this place," said Mitch.

"The rides aren't free though."

"We'll definitely be putting in an order. Thanks. You, uh, need help with that."

Paul looked down at himself. His throbbing member was green, far from climax. He turned back to the two humans. "I'm all right. Things are easier if I don't finish until after closing."

Mitch laughed. "Do you get a lot of new clients, or is it all just orders?"

"Most days I see at least one new person, but some days, yes... just filling orders."

"Must be a nice break."

"I like days like this." Paul stretched and sighed. "I'd prefer to be full all the time. My ideal day is to be full of new clients and all orders are for next day."

They laughed again.

"We made a mistake joining the Democratic Earth & Space Command," Mitch said. "We could have opened a shop like this."

"You think your mouth can memorize a dick?"

"I've got yours down pretty well." Mitch nudged the first man.

Smiling, they turned to leave. Paul waved goodbye. They turned and waved at him as they exited. Paul then turned to Aaza, who was just now standing up.

Aaza had been sitting in the corner, cup of coffee in one hand, tablet computer in the other. Weeks ago the wolflike ESC officer had brought in a table from Hadron's and set it there. Several times a week she sat for hours while Paul worked. Nobody seemed to notice her sipping coffee. Reading her tablet.

"I suppose I should report for my shift," she said, straightening her uniform. "Nice spending time with you, Paul."

Paul licked his lips. "Come back soon."

After a few tucks of her antistatic uniform, she strolled out. The door locked. Paul liked her. She wasn't put off by how he lived.

He figured an order or two was waiting, but he felt too good to get up right now. Paul stretched again and curled up, warm and content.

He'd seen a lot of new people in his shop in recent months. Many brand new species coming through the rift. Their scents were fascinating, and Paul had noticed a pattern among groups of species.

Here, avians tended to be thin and ropelike. Reptiles had ridges all up and down the shaft and tip. Felines tended to have stimulating barbs or bony protrusions on them.

Among the new species coming through the rift, everyone seemed to be thick and smooth, mammal, reptile, avian alike. He wondered if he should tell someone about this. Maybe it suggested a common ancestry. Maybe a common culture. It seemed unlikely, as this was supposed to be a whole other universe, but if it did mean something, that would imply...

Paul lost the thought.

He idly wished for more clients—more days like this, when he could be mounted one after another. Not too long after he had first opened the shop, he'd had several days like that in a row. Lots of Telosen and Atlins, one after the other. He had made so much money in his first month, more than enough to pay rent and buy food and cleaning beams.

Now that the ESC had taken over the station and the Atlin supervisors were gone, the shop rent had been cut in half, and operations had continued as usual, though it was no longer Telosen exhausted for days of customer service work. Now more people visited the station as a rest stop on longer journeys between the empires.

A matter/energy conversion beam interrupted his thoughts. Paul raised his head and turned to the door. A feathery canine was materializing at the entrance. Seconds later, he stood before Paul. His plumage was all reds and whites with a few yellows around the tips, most of it hidden underneath armor. Rather than a large suit covering his whole body, it was made of individual plates strapped tightly to him which seemed to emphasize his bulk. The muscles were larger than a Grovian's, and they looked swollen and bunched up even when not in motion. A vial of pink liquid was clipped to the chest, a small tube running into the clothes. He held a rifle in both hands.

"People of the Universe of Dead Water. I am second rank Lak'la'ta'an, and I speak on behalf of the Setjalar, servants of the Life. Their demands are simple. Everything through the rift is the territory of the Fluidic Province. Any vessels entering it will be considered trespassers and destroyed on sight. Any colony established in it will be considered ours to do with as we please. Any people found there will become ours to do with as we see fit. If you remain in your universe, no harm will come to you, and we can coexist in..."

Paul reluctantly rose from the bed and sat up, still out of his sheath and throbbing green. Lak'la'ta'an, turned to Paul and regarded him. Paul's tail wagged, and he scented the person from a distance. His scent was exquisite, and his appearance was pleasing to the eye as well.

Lak'la'ta'an's stately posture faltered as he looked around. Paul slid off the bed and stood up straight, still out of his sheath. The Setjalar looked at Paul as he approached, gun still held at ready.

"This is not the command center," said the feathered canine.

Paul's tail wagged as he stretched his neck and scented. "You're about fifty meters off to the side and ninety meters down."

"My... apologies then."

"Don't apologize." Paul had reached Lak'la'ta'an and was scenting him up close. The feathery canine remained rigid, as if standing in military formation. "I like meeting new species, and your scent is wonderful." Paul's erection changed from green to pink just taking in his scent. "A canine with feathers. Are you in military service, or do you have a warrior culture?"

"Third, recalibrate coordinates and send me to the command deck."

Paul sniffed his thick chest for another minute. The Setjalar seemed uneasy.

"Why is nothing happening?" Lak'la'ta'an said.

Paul had circled him and scented him from every angle. The armor covered most of his body, but his feathers still showed between the pieces. Paul knelt in front of the codpiece and concentrated on it. He didn't recognize what the armor was made of, but the feathers and body underneath smelled interesting.

"While you're here, would you like me to make you a profile?"

"I don't understand."

Paul placed a hand on Lak'la'ta'an's thigh, working his fingers between two armor plates and feeling the feathers.

"The universe has some scary diseases. Most of the people share a common biology, so they are sometimes vulnerable to the same viruses. I've made profiles of a number of people from your universe, and I've found some common features. I will guess you can be affected by them, too."

Lak'la'ta'an remained rigid and at attention, looking down at Paul. "Our reconnaissance did not report on this. What sort of diseases?"

Paul embraced his thigh, rubbing his chin against the codpiece. The feathers did not hide the muscles at all. "Mmmmm, keep searching. You'll find out. I can help."

"The Life will research this and find ways to protect us from them in time."

Paul reached around and felt his rear plate covering the hamstring. He managed to work his hand underneath it. Paul looked up at him. He could just barely see the canine's face between his chest muscles, which stuck out far enough to be a shelf Paul could stand on.

"Lots of people could become sick in the meantime. I can give you a head start."

The Setjalar seemed uneasy in his stance. "Something strange is happening. What are you doing to me? Who are you?"

"My name is Paul. I run this shop."

"And how can you help us?"

"Let me build a profile of you, and I will show you."

He lost his military stance. "Something is..." He reached down and unclipped the codpiece. It fell away and dangled between his thighs, revealing a slit and a bright orange tip peeking from it. Lak'la'ta'an had bent down, straining to see himself between his pectorals. "What is that? This has... this has never happened before. What are you doing to me?"

Paul was scenting it. "Oooooh, you smell so nice."

"What is happening?"

Paul looked up at him. "You really don't know?"

"The Setjalar are bred to be soldiers of the Fluidic Province. This is... This is something I have not experienced before."

Paul took a chance and gave the tip a quick lick. The Setjalar shivered and lowered his weapon. He slid further out of his slit, revealing an organ that resembled a canine's, as long as Paul's forearm, and it had an intricate pattern of grooves and subtle ridges, like a human's fingerprint wrapping around it. The texture intrigued Paul—he had encountered nothing like it on any client previously.

"A canine with feathers and a reptile slit but a canine organ," Paul said, nuzzling it. "Are you a..." He hesitated. Talking about it was still difficult for him. "Are you a Construct, too?"

"I do not understand."

"Please allow me to build a profile of you, and then I will show you how you can protect yourself from the various diseases in this universe."

Lak'la'ta'an held his weapon at his side, looking down at Paul and the orange piece of skin coming from his body. He seemed scared of it.

"Very well."

Paul instantly swung his muzzle and took it all the way. His eyes had been right. The entire shaft and head was covered in a fingerprint pattern, like a labyrinth, no lines touching, seemingly no beginning or end, creating a single path winding and wrapping and folding and weaving around and around, side to side—if he unfolded the path, it would be long enough to encircle the station. Paul closed his eyes. He needed some extra time to learn this.

Lak'la'ta'an stood still, trying to remain disciplined and at attention, but these sensations must have been new to him as well, as he did not know what to do. Paul felt privileged to be someone's first.

Finally Paul had memorized the contours. He released him and stood up. Paul noticed his own organ had changed to black, very near climax. Studying this new species had almost pushed him over the edge. Finishing while building a profile would have been unprofessional, but he doubted this Setjalar would have cared.

"Lak'la'ta'an," Paul began, "you have a beautiful organ."

"Is that what it is called?"

"You said you were bred to be soldiers, so why do you have this? Are you..." Paul hesitated again. "Are you not a natural life form? Did someone construct you?"

"The Life designed us to be their soldiers."

"I thought so. Well, I will guess someone decided to be creative with your genes. They left you with a penis, and they gave you a beautiful pattern of ridges."

Paul turned and walked to the far door. To his surprise, the Setjalar followed him from a close distance, still holding his rifle. Paul stood at the terminal and selected a base shape to work with. Lak'la'ta'an stood over his shoulder, observing.

"What are you doing?"

Paul normally didn't allow clients in here, but Lak'la'ta'an was special.

"I will build a profile of it and make you a protective sleeve."

"And this will protect us from diseases in the Universe of Dead Water?"

"You won't find better protection."

Paul began adjusting the curves and typing numbers. He typed a string of numbers one after the other, fingers flying over the terminal screen. Before their eyes, the basic shape of the profile on screen lengthened and morphed until it resembled Lak'la'ta'an's.

"You are not a natural life form either, Paul?"

Paul's ears turned backwards. "No, I'm not."

"For what purpose were you constructed? You are clearly not a soldier."

Paul now began creating the fingerprint pattern. He knew how he could do it, and he hoped the feathered canine wouldn't mind the wait. He set the model to rotate at a specific rate, and Paul traced the pattern with one finger as a single line going around and over the shaft, moving his finger side to side slightly to denote the subtle differences in width he had observed.

"I was never a soldier. I was a... a project."

"A prototype, then. Our reconnaissance was unaware species in this universe practiced such techniques. I must inform my superiors."

"I wasn't a prototype soldier."

"For what purpose were you created?"

"I was released before anyone could tell me."

"A possible military experiment. Perhaps an incomplete one. We may be forced to address this scenario in the future."

The phallus on screen was rotating about three times per second. The fine line Paul was tracing on it became visible now, and Lak'la'ta'an must have just noticed.

"How are you doing this?"

"I learned how to translate information in my head into computer commands. Your pattern is actually quite relaxing to trace."

"You process information far faster than any we have observed. Your construction must have had military applications. It is unfortunate you were unable to fulfill your purpose."

Paul liked breathing Lak'la'ta'an's scent. It filled the small room and relaxed him in a way he had not felt since Akaak. It had been months since he'd thought of that Grovian. Paul was happy to know a resin replica of gres sex organ was preserved in the chamber of the council, where it commemorated the battle that had taken gres life and thus restored honor to the House. It was the most popular warrior relic on display. Paul had been told the Grovians always included him in the story of how this relic survived the battle, making Paul famous on Grovi.

Paul finished the labyrinth. He had replicated the pattern exactly, even taking into account the varying height and width of the grooves along the way. Paul felt proud of himself for being able to recreate it in one try.

He sent it to the printer. The machine behind them whirred to life and began molding the sleeve. Lak'la'ta'an turned and faced it, rifle held at ready.

"It's just making your prototype."

A moment of silence, and then Lak'la'ta'an turned to him. "This has been valuable reconnaissance, albeit unexpected. You have shown your willingness to help the Life for the good of the Fluidic Province. I will inform my First about your services."

"I hope to meet others of your kind. I wonder if they all smell as good as you do."

"Smell?"

"My senses are artificially heightened."

"Mine are as well, though I do not believe my tongue could be as accurate as a computer system. My eyes have been enhanced to improve my aim with a rifle. My muscles are enhanced to ensure I can overpower an enemy in close combat. I lack a digestive system, fed instead by the Life in the form of a nutrient solution." He pointed to the vial clipped to his chest plate.

Paul looked at him as the machine hummed. The canine's feathers had settled, and they hugged the muscles even better. Normally the smell of polymer overpowered anything else in the room, but Lak'la'ta'an's scent still remained strong. Paul glanced down. The Setjalar's organ was still out, solid, and emitting quite an enticing odor.

Paul met the feathered canine's eyes. "Were you created as an adult, or did you have to grow up?"

"I emerged from a tank as I am now."

"So did I. I'm curious. What was your first thought?"

"My clearest memory after emerging from the tank was being assigned the rank of Third and sent to a division."

"My first thought was to raise my tail for the first person I smelled."

"I do not understand."

"Your reconnaissance did not tell you about that?"

"If it did, the Life did not divulge it to us. The Setjalar need only know enough to carry out their orders. Obedience brings victory, and victory is our purpose."

A rolled up piece of polymer emerged from the machine. Paul took it and led the feathery dog out of the room.

"I'll show you, and how this will protect you from the universe's diseases."

"I will comply, for the good of the Fluidic Province and in service to the Life."

Paul led the way to the bed and turned around. He was still out of his sheath and throbbing, penis a deep black. Lak'la'ta'an stared at it as he approached.

"You possess an organ as well. It looks nothing like mine. You will show me its purpose?"

Paul's tail wagged. "Step closer."

He stopped, standing at military attention again. He was still out of his slit. Paul lined the sleeve up with the top of the shaft and rolled it down. The sleeve fell into the grooves and locked in place, practically disappearing.

Lak'la'ta'an dropped his rifle. It clattered on the carpet and came to a harmless rest. He reached down and felt Paul's muzzle.

"What is happening?"

Paul turned around and leaned over the bed, tail up and waving gently from side to side. Normally he'd already be filled. Paul looked back, and the armored canine merely stared. He looked at Paul's rear but did not seem to know what happened next.

Paul patted his left hip.

The Setjalar remained stationary.

"Put it in."

The canine took a step forward and gripped Paul's hips with both hands. His biceps puckered his already-bulky chest, visible even under his armor and plumage, and Paul's tail wagged. Paul looked ahead and waited. He felt a tip poking him and waited another breath. Smiling, Paul pushed his hips backwards and was instantly filled all the way. Now he rose to full height and stood hip to hip with the canine. His arms squeezed Paul's face. Paul whimpered, reminded of all the times he'd been with Grovians.

Lak'la'ta'an stood still.

Paul moved his hips, pulling him out, and then pushing it back in.

That must have done it.

Suddenly Lak'la'ta'an fell from his soldier posture and pushed Paul back over the bed. He pulled halfway out and pushed all the way back in, testing it. The guttural sounds that came from his throat made Paul raise his tail higher.

"Go as hard as you want."

Lak'la'ta'an did. He thrust fast and deep, trying different angles, different depths, clutching Paul's hips as if afraid the scaliefox would try to escape. He was thrusting so hard he was pushing Paul up onto the bed. Eventually he was face down on it, Lak'la'ta'an lying on Paul, still buried all the way to the hilt. If not for the weight and shape of the organ, Paul could have imagined being under a Telosen.

He had paused. Paul did not open his eyes as he spoke. "This... This is... You are not injured?"

"Mmmmmmmm no. You feel so good in me."

"I wish... I wish to continue."

"Do anything you want to me."

Lak'la'ta'an pulled out again and slowly pushed back in. This made him shudder, and he rose halfway up and thrust deep but lightly. With the weight off his back, Paul breathed easier, and now he only felt weight on his hips.

He was moving faster now, still remaining deep, and with more passion than Paul expected. Now he was feeling the fur on Paul's back as he moved. His hand wandered up to Paul's face, and he felt the scales lining his muzzle. Paul leaned into his touch. Lak'la'ta'an sped up, but the angle didn't feel right anymore.

He rose to all fours, and now Lak'la'ta'an lay on him and thrust, holding Paul around the chest. This gave him much more leverage, and he thrust deep, gradually speeding up. Paul felt a knot swelling, and he was glad the polymer could expand to accommodate.

Lak'la'ta'an's hand wandered down his stomach and then gripped Paul's organ. The touch made Paul climax, and Lak'la'ta'an felt it all around as it pulsed, even moving to feel the liquid coming out. Paul's productivity was just as exaggerated as his reproductive organs. Whenever he reached climax, he pulsed for several minutes, releasing enormous quantities of seed. Paul liked when people touched him during his climax, and the feathered canine seemed fascinated by what Paul's body was doing. Lak'la'ta'an didn't seem to be aware he was speeding up, but he held Paul tighter the faster he did.

He growled. He snarled. He squeezed Paul's chest.

Now he thrust so hard Paul couldn't stay on his hands and knees, and he fell to the mattress. Lak'la'ta'an practically held Paul up to his chest while he thrust as fast as he could, apparently no longer exploring but milking as much feeling out of this as possible.

One last throaty snarl, and Lak'la'ta'an shuddered. His thrusting stopped. A moment went by. Paul wished he could feel it in him. He wanted to know how warm a Setjalar's seed was.

Lak'la'ta'an slowly pulled out and looked at himself. "That was... Remarkably different."

Paul panted and rolled over to face him, cock pulsing and seed still spurting out. He had soaked the covers already. He held Lak'la'ta'an's feathery muzzle, wishing the armor wasn't between them. Lak'la'ta'an leaned over Paul and wrapped his arms around the scaliefox.

"Why am I behaving this way?"

Paul breathed his scent as his arm muscles squeezed him. Lak'la'ta'an's arm was as thick as Paul's torso. "Maybe an instinct your makers couldn't cut out of your genes. You should remove the sleeve before you retract."

"Remove?"

Paul's tail beat the bed, and he reached down and peeled the polymer off. It had already retracted halfway. Paul set it gently on the edge of the bed and reached around him, hoping Lak'la'ta'an would remove the rest of his armor. Lak'la'ta'an lay on top of Paul, snout to snout with him.

"And..." Lak'la'ta'an began, "these devices will keep us safe from disease?"

"They will, and I make them so they will never slip off or break."

"How many can you produce in an hour's time?"

"About three hundred."

"The Fluidic Province will need as many as we are able to obtain. Do you consent to being transported aboard our vessel, equipment and all?"

"No, I'm happy here. Plenty of other people who need help. I made fifty extra copies for you. No charge this time."

"I urge you to reconsider. You may be a valuable asset for the Life."

The door chime sounded. Paul ignored it, but then he heard a secondary chime. The commander and Cylinder were the only two people on the station who could override Paul's lock. Paul turned his head and faced the door.

Commander Blunt and Cylinder stormed in, laser rifles pointed straight at the bed. Z-rank Sela Jar'i and Lieutenant Aaza Kas-sti followed, holding hand lasers. Cylinder had taken a spherical form.

"Commander Blunt," Paul said. "I was showing Lak'la'ta'an how the sleeves work."

The canine suddenly became a soldier again. He climbed off the bed, grabbing his rifle, and stood at attention, codpiece still dangling against his thigh. He had retracted into his slit completely, so apart from some liquid dripping from it, he looked stately.

"Greetings, civilians and soldiers of the Universe of Dead Water," he began. "I am Second rank Lak'la'ta'an, and I speak on behalf of the Setjalar, servants of the Life."

Paul rolled to his back while Lak'la'ta'an gave his speech again. His penis had finally stopped pumping seed everywhere and had begun to retract. Paul stared dreamily up at the ceiling, drinking his scent. He wondered who had constructed his species. They must have been scent-based.

He and the commander exchanged tough words, and then finally he announced his intent. Paul heard a conversion beam and turned to see. Lak'la'ta'an was looking at him from the corner of his eye. Paul waved goodbye as he dematerialized and was teleported off the station.

The crew ran into the room, scanning, taking readings. Aaza held a scanner up to the bed.

"Trace amounts of DNA everywhere. Not enough to sequence, and we'll never separate it from all the other traces."

Paul gestured to the used sleeve. "Here's a sample."

She smirked and walked over to it. "Very substantial DNA sample here. Gametic cells, but potentially useful. We should take it to Doctor Dorset for him to analyze the way only a heterosexual white man can."

Paul felt a human kneeling over him. Commander Blunt. "Paul, what happened?"

"He beamed in. He was a wonderful client."

"That was more than an hour ago. He was here that long?"

"He lasted a long time, and he felt good in me, and he smelled so nice. I haven't enjoyed a client like that since Akaak."

"Paul, the entire station was under siege! That Setjalar came to deliver terms, and you've been sleeping with him the whole time?"

"Uh huh."

"Didn't you listen to his speech?"

"He didn't say anything about you. He only did the first part. That's when he realized he was in the wrong place."

The wolf rose from the bed, holding the used sleeve between her claws. "Commander, I think we have all we need."

Blunt stood up and addressed the room. "The Fluidic Province is out there, and when they come, this station will be the first thing they try to take. We'll be ready."

Paul wondered who he was talking to. He yawned and felt his own rear, sometimes imagining a Grovian pressing against him, sometimes imagining a Setjalar.

INT – PAUL'S SHOP / 0300

Paul woke up in the middle of the night. He rose from the bed and stretched. Barely able to walk after helping so many clients and spending so much time teaching Lak'la'ta'an how his penis worked, he stumbled to the printer. He looked at the conveyor belt. Empty. Paul pressed a few buttons and ran off one more copy. As soon as it came out, a conversion beam fell over it, and it vanished. Paul's tail wagged. He queued another fifty copies.

He checked the terminal. Eleven orders to print, all due later today. He walked to the other wall and used a credit to make himself a modest meal. When he came back, the fiftieth one dropped onto the belt.

A non-ESC conversion beam washed over all of them, and the whole lot vanished. Another beam hit the belt, and three vials of pink liquid appeared. Paul took one and examined it. He guessed this meant he had fulfilled his largest single order request yet.

He held the vial up to his chest and sighed. It had scents of other Setjalar on it. Paul climaxed as he sniffed one after another. He made sure to aim away from the printer. It lasted for several minutes, and he became a fountain pulsing seed for the second time today. The puddle on the floor grew to a lake as Paul thought of that wonderful profile inside him.

4

INT — HADRON'S BAR / 0840

Unlike his colleagues on Far Space 3, back when it was a Customer Support Station, Hadron had learned the value of outstanding appearances and superlative customer experience. As a hatchling, he had been raised to believe in the unquestioning value of these things, and as a result, he had never flagged in the system for improper expressions or vocal inflections. When he was allowed to retire, he set up a shop in the station, giving encouragement and even coaching to some of the avians who needed help recovering from dealing with customers all day.

When Telose revolted against being the face of Atlin customer support, Hadron had not joined. He didn't understand what the revolt was about. All he saw was a station full of representatives who didn't really believe in what they were doing and couldn't follow the rules.

Hadron purchased a new outfit every week. The one he wore this week was styled after a human fashion trend. He'd been told it was a prostitute's outfit from a different century, but it worked very well for him, as it covered his legs. The lace was tricky to work, but it produced a unique result. Among species who wore clothing, certain coverings came with connotations. Hadron was determined to shatter them.

Careful not to stumble while wearing high-heels, Hadron climbed the stairs, two bottles in hand, looking out over the tables. The muscular T-rexes sat and stood around his bar, most staring into space. The saurians only wore their traditional waistcovers, made of metal and decorated with dangling chains, some with claws and teeth and pieces of dried skin hanging from them, relics of ancestors who had died in battle. Some were sharpening their claws.

The bird had reached the top of the stairs and walked to where Doctor Dorset and Systems Update Specialist Ihara were sitting. He stood between the two ESC officers.

"Good afternoon, gentlemen of the Democratic Earth & Space Command Committed to Peace and Democracy. Here for a drink?"

The thin lizard waved him off. "No, we're just here for a heterosexual chat."

The human nodded. "That's right. We come here often for our heterosexual chats."

"On the house. I insist." He began pouring them glasses of reddish liquid, leaning in between them. He lowered his voice. "In exchange for a little information. What in the name of the Laws of Customer Experience is going on? I wake up and the whole station is swarming with Grovians."

Doctor Dorset, the human, leaned in close, also lowering his voice. "Apparently an armada of ships was passing this way and the commander gave them permission to come aboard for a little R and R."

He poured them a little more. "Do you really believe that?"

"Why else would they be here?" Ihara asked.

"Listen." Hadron paused, looked left, right. "Twenty-nine decibels. I've served a lot of Grovians over the years. A group of ten raises the noise level to eighty *while sober*. I stopped counting the number of lizards on this station when I hit forty. I hate to put it this way, but it is too quiet."

"It's rather pleasant I think," Dorset said.

"Something's wrong," the avian said, shaking his head. "Take that to Blunt for me, please. The Grovians are up to something. If I hear any loose talk, I'll let you know."

Ihara picked up the half-full glass. "Likewise. Thanks for the drink before my shift."

"Well, the last firmware update made you lose your clutch, so it's safe to drink now," said the doctor.

Ihara raised his glass in reply. He enjoyed sharing heterosexual humor with fellow heterosexuals.

In fact, the ESC had pushed an update to the shield generator software the other week, and somehow it broke the code that operated the doors on the station. Ihara and his team had to manually open doors for people until version 18.6.1.2.2b came out.

"I think I'll have one myself," Hadron said. "And just for good measure, I'll join Aaza in Paul's shop."

The bird capped the bottle and walked away. Ihara clinked glasses with Dorset and took a sip. They both looked around, now conscious of the quiet, and then resumed their heterosexual conversation.

INT – COMMAND DECK / 1100

Commander Blunt stood beside the wolf. She displayed a map of sensor sweeps over the last three hours. Some of the Grovian ships had been breaking off and were circling the station in a patrol pattern. Several others were making wider rings around the station.

"No doubt about it, sir," Aaza said. "They're setting up a perimeter around the solar system."

The commander stared at the screen. "R and R indeed. Any idea what they want?"

"Can't tell. You didn't get any answers from Uzhok?"

"All urm told me was that war was coming."

Z-rank Sela Jar'i turned from the screen and faced the commander. "No Province ships have come through in months."

"They're here," Blunt said. "They're figuring out what their next move is."

Sela's feathers rose. "Maybe the Grovians found them and they're getting ready to draw first blood."

"We shouldn't speculate. None of the Grovians appear to be talking."

Aaza smirked. "With this many reptiles on the station you'd think one of them would get drunk enough to talk." Her station chimed. "Commander, we're receiving four distress calls, all from freighters leaving the station. The Grovians are not allowing anyone to pass."

"Open a channel to the Grovian ships."

"Open, sir."

"This is Commander Adrian Blunt of Far Space 3. This system is under the jurisdiction of the Democratic Earth & Space Command Committed to Peace and Democracy. You are not authorized to patrol here. State your purpose."

Aaza: "One response. Routing it through."

A saurian face with green scales and white highlights on the ridges appeared on screen. "Commander, we are under orders to form a blockade around the station and the rift. No vessels are permitted to enter or leave until further notice."

Blunt narrowed his eyes, though the gesture would be lost on a reptilian species. "On whose authority?"

"The Grovian council."

"What's going on?"

"That should be obvious."

Commander Blunt stepped a little closer to the screen. The reptile would understand it as a challenging gesture. "The Grovian government does not have jurisdiction here."

The reptile leaned closer to the screen. "Look around you, Commander. The Fluidic Province has been coming through the rift for years, spying on us, learning our weaknesses. What have we learned of them? It's time to stop waiting for war to come and realize the enemy is already here."

The human pushed a few keys on Aaza Kas-sti's terminal, alerting the Rebel to prepare for departure. "This is your last warning. Let those ships go and halt your patrols, or I will come there and do it for you."

"It is no longer a time of peace."

The screen went blank.

Commander Blunt turned and marched to the lift. "Z-rank Sela, you have the station. The rest of you, meet me on the Rebel in five minutes."

Five paces before reaching the lift, Commander Blunt halted.

"Wait..."

Aaza was still at her console, about to follow. She was staring. "Something wrong, sir?"

Blunt turned and faced them. "Why are we wasting our time going on a dangerous space mission when there's a perfectly good solution right here on this station?"

Aaza looked at the others. They seemed just as confused.

EXT – ESTABLISHING SHOT: THE STARSHIP REBEL NOT UNDOCKING FROM FARS3'S OUTER DIAMOND

INT – PAUL'S SHOP / 1109

Paul watched the image of Commander Blunt on the viewscreen of his console.

"The Grovians have caged us. They refuse to tell us why, and there are too many vessels to risk an open conflict. We need information, and..."

Paul heard his words but they barely registered. Paul idly wondered how Commander Blunt's penis would feel in his mouth. All these years and he still hadn't seen it.

"...I have already been in shouting matches with several Grovians. Nobody on my staff can get any answers out of them. I considered petitioning the ESC to send its only Grovian officer to the station in the hopes je would be able to get someone to talk about their intentions, but that would likely be contrived and expensive. Hadron and several others have instructions to send you clients. You may be inundated with Grovians."

The scaliefox nodded as he reached behind himself and felt his rear. Just the thought of Grovians again...

"...I had considered taking the Rebel out and intercepting the Grovians, but that would probably just be too dramatic. Much easier to enlist you. If anyone can get the Grovians talking, it's you, Paul. Can I count on you?"

Paul imagined Blunt's organ must be a variation on the human profile, likely with the skin on the tip intact, so that left length and width and bend as the primary variables...

"Yes, commander, I understand."

Paul walked back to the new bed. The room had three beds and two chairs in it now. The new bed was a standard ESC issue, and the new chair was Eneg.

He lay with his rear facing the door. No orders to print right now. He had no idea there were so many Grovians on the station, and now he waited for Hadron's staff to send him clients. His tail wagged at the thought of Grovians.

Minutes later, a Grovian stepped through the door. Then another. Then another, this last one with several teeth and claws dangling from gres waistcover. Their arms alone were about half as thick as Paul's body. The Construct rolled over and sat on his knees, oversized, scaly sheath and testicles squished against the mattress. His purple tip peeked from his sheath just at the sight of three Grovians.

"Welcome, members of great Houses."

They seemed unmoved by the traditional greeting. They were scenting the room and Paul from a distance. Paul slid off the bed and approached, making sure his junk jiggled.

"Hadron suggested we visit," the one on the left said.

"My name is Paul. Did he tell you what to expect?"

Je parted his jaws, showing gres teeth in a sly smile. "He informed us. He also informed us of the consequences of getting out of line."

"Good." Paul was among them now. They surrounded him on three sides. "Then he must have told you three you may do anything you want to me, but only after you're wearing one of my sleeves."

"I'm curious," said the one on his right.

"Remove your clothes, and I will show you."

The three saurians exchanged glances, and then all at once they unclamped the metal around their waists. They set them down and closed in. Paul only had two hands, so this would require some coordination, but he had juggled five clients at once before.

Paul began rubbing two of their slits. They grunted and growled, and ridged tips emerged from two of them. Paul then began rubbing the other. Moments later, he had three Grovian organs poking his muzzle.

He chose the one who had teeth hanging from gres waistcover first. Paul opened his muzzle and took urm down his throat, letting his tongue trace the contours and convert them into information the computer would understand.

The Grovian stood still, looking down at Paul, other hand on gres hip, amused and delighted. Meanwhile Paul was rubbing the slits of the other two. It didn't take long to build a mental map of the contours, and Paul released urm, adjusting his stance to the second bipedal lizard. Paul was tempted to reach up and feel their abs and arms while he did this, but he didn't want to encourage them to do anything yet.

The second lizard was about the same size and shape, but the ridges were deeper. Paul mapped them in no time, and then he moved to the third, using his hands to keep the other two stimulated. They stood still and grunted and growled. Paul glimpsed them bumping muzzles.

Paul had profiles of all three of them. Everyone seemed so easy now after the Setjalar. Not disappointing, but Paul was wondering if he would ever meet someone he couldn't map.

The Grovians stood to the side and let him up. He noted they were looking at one another, making noises Paul did not understand. It was probably the first time they had seen one another naked and hard—the first time any of them had seen what was in the other's slit.

"Give me a few moments to make your prototypes, and then you may try them out. Feel free to have a seat anywhere."

Paul walked to the back and left the three of them alone. He stood at the terminal and pulled up the standard template for a Grovian. The variations were easy to enter into the system, and less than five minutes later, Paul had sent the order to the printer. He printed three copies of each rather than the usual single sample.

He looked down at himself and noticed his cock had changed from purple to red. He was getting worked up just thinking about three Grovians one after the other.

Three sets of three rolled sleeves emerged from the printer. Paul collected them and walked out. The saurians had all taken seats on the Grovian chair, all three still out of their slits, looking at one another, speaking in their native language.

Paul approached and handed two rolled sleeves to each. The third he slipped over them one at a time.

"How's that?" Paul said.

The sleeves contoured to their ridges. The one on the left was feeling it up and down, marveling at how well it stayed in place. The saurians were still talking amongst themselves in their own language. Paul wondered what the command to turn off the station's automatic translator was.

Now Paul leaned over and felt their abs and bulging arms. The one who had had claws and teeth hanging from gres waistcover pulled Paul down to gres chest and held him there. Paul guessed je was the highest ranking of the three. His fingers wandered up gres chest—he would have needed three hands to span each pectoral. Je wrapped both arms around Paul and squeezed him, and Paul lay his muzzle between gres chest muscles, looking straight at a predatory gaze. Paul heard the other two getting up.

"No lubricants needed," Paul said. "I make my own. I'm designed for this."

Paul held on. Every single saurian he had ever been with had a hard, unyielding body, and he loved it when they used him in groups. He felt a pair of clawed hands on his hips and pressure under his tail. He recognized who was sliding into him by the shape of gres organ.

Je was a fast and hard partner, and Paul held the ranking Grovian around gres shoulders while the one behind him pushed all the way in. The growls and grunts pushed Paul closer to climax more than the feeling of being full.

He kept eye contact with the ranking Grovian while the other grabbed his hips and thrust. Paul felt gres face.

That predatory gaze never softened, and je kept Paul in a tight grip.

The one behind him gripped his rear so hard Paul felt claws. The heat of gres organ went through the sleeve and straight to Paul's heart. Je sped up. The ranking Grovian nuzzled Paul as the subordinate used him. Paul nuzzled urm back, licking gres muzzle a few times. Je licked Paul, though Grovians had no such gesture for affection.

Moments later, the second-ranking Grovian slowed down and grunted, squeezing Paul's rear. Paul felt gres pulsing inside him. He closed his eyes and panted. The ranking Grovian scented his breath and licked his muzzle.

Je pulled out. The ranking Grovian pulled Paul closer to gres face. Paul rubbed muzzles with urm, and je nuzzled Paul. Gres hands wandered around Paul's body. Je looked down Paul's body from several angles as the third Grovian pushed inside.

Paul closed his eyes and lay on the ranking Grovian. He always enjoyed using larger species for a bed. Something so comforting about it. He felt every twitch of every muscle as this Grovian adjusted him for the third saurian. Paul wondered if these three knew one another, or if they were related.

Number three pushed in, and Paul felt every single ridge—shallower than the second Grovian, but much more intricate. Paul buried his muzzle in the ranking saurian's solid chest and felt gres arms.

Je was a much slower partner, and Paul liked it when they lasted longer. He opened his eyes. The ranking lizard was looking straight at him, now feeling down the line where his scales changed to fur.

"What are you?" je asked.

Paul panted a few times. "I'm a Construct."

The lead Grovian grunted at that and bumped Paul's muzzle with gres. The thrusting pushed him up closer to the muzzle. Only gres thick arms held him in place.

Grovian three was taking a long time to finish. The second Grovian had taken a seat next to the ranking one, Paul's bed.

They tapped muzzles and looked Paul over.

Number three began to speed up. Paul felt another hand on him, feeling his fur. The more hands on him, the closer Paul came to finishing.

Paul looked back and forth between the sets of eyes studying him. Two predatory gazes. He rubbed his nose against theirs whenever one was close enough.

Pulsing inside him, and Paul finished all over the lead Grovian's stomach. Je felt it and realized it wasn't a typical climax, as it didn't let up. Je opened gres mouth, held Paul's muzzle in gres, and gently shook him side to side.

Number three pulled out. Paul gasped and whimpered, practically begging to feel this one inside him while he was still pulsing. Je sat up straight, releasing Paul but still keeping a good hold on him. Paul wagged his tail as he squirted three more times. Gres stomach and chest were covered. The other two Grovians moved in, sniffing it and licked it up, but more was still coming out. All three Grovians looked at one another, obviously taken aback. They licked Paul's scales clean and tried to catch as much as they could.

The ranking Grovian held Paul in gres lap. He felt gres sleeved organ against his back. Je lifted Paul up over gres head. Paul watched gres muscles pucker and bulk out as his cock continued to pulse and cover the saurian's stomach and chest. The other two were trying to keep up with the fountain. Je slowly lowered Paul over gres organ. It spread Paul out, and the ridges brushed against him in one, smooth motion until he sat on urm.

Je let go of Paul and rested gres arms for the first time since they had begun. Paul braced himself on gres shoulders and lifted himself up and then sat down again. So rare for a client to give him control, and Paul cherished it. He took the chance to feel gres arms all the way down as he rode urm, the lines between each muscle becoming deeper and more pronounced.

By now the other two had taken a seat next to their ranking officer. Eldest brother perhaps, either by blood or battlefield bond. They were feeling Paul's scales while his underside was exposed. A species having both scales and fur like this must have fascinated them, and they continued to remark on the sight of Paul's unceasing climax. They lapped it up from the ranking Grovian's stomach and took turns trying to capture it as it came out.

While he slid back down, Paul reached out and felt their muzzles. They regarded him as they felt his belly and chest, so soft and minuscule compared to theirs. The lead Grovian leaned back and let Paul ride urm as he pleased, eyes fixed on Paul's continuing climax. Paul felt gres chest and shoulders on his way up, and then let his hands wander to gres stomach on his way down, cupping each individual abdominal as they flexed with gres panting.

The ridges rubbed Paul perfectly. The other two Grovians were mumbling to one another as they lapped up everything Paul produced. The touches made Paul ride faster. The ranking Grovian looked up at the ceiling, growling.

Both managed to follow Paul's cock as he rode this lizard, but the two saurians were unable to keep up with the flow. They laughed as it began to cover their muzzles, and they let it happen, surrendering. Gradually, Paul's cock slowed, and he stopped releasing. He had covered three Grovians.

His partner's hips began to thrust. Gradually an arm wrapped around Paul and held him to gres chest. Je took control and began thrusting Paul deeper and harder.

Paul felt pulsing under his tail. He felt content to sit still and let urm finish. Je grunted and struggled to speak.

"You were designed for this?"

"I was."

"I can tell."

Paul rubbed the furred part of his muzzle against urm, raising his snout and also letting urm feel the scales. Je seemed to like the presence of both at once.

"There's a lot of Grovians on the station lately," Paul said. "What's the occasion?"

All three laughed.

"War is coming," said the second. "We are here to meet it."

Paul rubbed himself against his partner, marveling at how rigid the Grovian body was. "What war?"

They laughed again. Paul's partner picked him up and raised him off gres tool. Je pulled the sleeve off and then deposited Paul back on gres lap, engorged member just beginning to retract. The other two both leaned over outside of Paul's field of view and licked it.

After a few more minutes of basking in the climax, je lifted Paul up and carried him across the room. Paul curled up in gres arms, nuzzling a bicep as large as Paul's head, and then je deposited Paul on the bed. One by one each Grovian came up to Paul and held his muzzle with their teeth, just barely poking the skin, and then turned to leave, the ranking Grovian licking some of the semen off the other two as they walked.

Paul lay flat on his back and caught his breath. Ten minutes later, he heard three orders ping in the system. Paul couldn't let himself fall asleep this time; he was on assignment. He rolled to his feet and walked to the desk. He pushed the button.

"Paul to Commander Blunt."

Go ahead, came a voice over the com.

"First three Grovians stopped by. No news yet, but my ears are open."

Acknowledged.

EXT – FARS3, GROVIAN VESSELS DOCKED WITH AND ENCIRCLING IT

INT – PAUL'S SHOP / 1930

Paul hadn't locked the door in days. The stream of business was too fast, and the room was packed with T-Rexes, most of whom were lounging or walking about naked and hard, others merely stood by and watched, amused at all the dicks on display and Paul being mounted one after the other. It tempted Paul to believe those were the women, but some of them eventually stepped forward and undid their metal waistcovers to reveal an organ for Paul to map. Something about the air in here lately. Nobody could stay in their slits long.

Paul had been out of his sheath all day and climaxed three more times. Cleaning up after just one of his climaxes was difficult and expensive, as the special conversion beams were not complimentary. The beams did a wonderful job teleporting unwanted substances out of fabrics and carpet and leaving everything else in place. Paul kept his fur and scales clean free of charge thanks to the conversation beam showers, which were free.

It was so crowded in here Hadron had called him and asked if he needed catering services. The scaliefox had declined the offer.

Paul lay on the bed. The Grovian lay on top of him. Je seemed to like hearing Paul gasp under gres weight. Je used Paul quickly and deep, and then je pulled out. Paul had just barely risen to his hands and knees when the next Grovian stepped up behind and pushed in. Paul hung his head and gasped. He knew exactly who it was by the asymmetry of the ridges, and they felt just as wonderful under his tail as they had against his tongue.

More Grovians stepped in. They took positions against the wall and observed. Paul heard someone explain the rules to them, and they leaned back and watched. Paul heard something that caught his ear. He kept his ear from swiveling so he wouldn't alert urm.

He focused on Aaza, at her table in the corner. No coffee today. She was drinking Stozi wine, and she rarely looked up from her tablet no matter how loud it become in here. Paul wondered what she was reading.

INT – PAUL'S SHOP / 1845

The door chime rang. Paul was too tired to take any new clients and had set the door to leave an automated notice that CCS was closed for the night. Moments later, the override alert roused him from the Telose bed, and Paul rolled to his side and faced the commander, making no effort whatsoever to cover himself.

Blunt parted the curtain and stood just inside the door. "I wanted to bring you up to speed on what's been happening these last few days. The Grovians have abandoned their plan to steal Far Space 3 and take it inside the rift."

"That's good."

Blunt smiled. "You missed a great adventure, Paul. Shortly after we confronted the Grovians with their plan, they stormed the station. You must have been asleep. Somehow they got a hold of the research Doctor Resho did on

Cylinder. Specifically, the section that described Cylinder being able to live inside someone's body for extended periods, keeping them hydrated and filtering the blood so there is no need for restroom breaks for days at a time. The Grovians became convinced the Life is hiding everywhere. Everyone was now their enemy. We fought back, and then half the fleet set course for the Stozi and Atlin empires. They were going to use this as an excuse to expand their territory. Some had volunteered to collapse the rift and strand themselves on the other side to begin a generational campaign to find the Province's home planet."

"Life?" Paul said. He scratched his sheath, though he did not have an itch there.

"You didn't know? We learned about that over a year ago."

"Nobody's mentioned them to me."

Blunt laughed. Paul reached down and nudged his sac, making his oversized testicles bounce.

"You really do need to get out more," the commander said. "We found out Cylinder's species is the Life. They founded the Fluidic Province, and they've been on a campaign of conquest ever since they discovered our universe. We're not exactly sure what they want or why they seem beyond reason. Even Cylinder hasn't had any success talking to them."

"Hmmm..." Paul rolled to his back.

"An invasion is on the horizon, Paul. You have to be ready to evacuate if something happens."

"I'll be fine here."

"Paul, when the Fluidic Province comes, they may throw you in prison or worse."

"Nobody would hurt me. Everyone likes me."

The commander chuckled and shook his head. "Be that as it may, have a plan."

Paul's tail wagged. "I promise."

"Anyway, thank you for helping us deal with the Grovians. Nothing like a little rest and relaxation to mellow out that warrior spirit and get them talking. That's the problem with a warrior culture. If there is no war to fight, they have to go looking for fights. You saved thousands, if not millions of Grovians from needlessly sacrificing themselves. Their paranoia would have been an excuse to invade every planet for generations. The Grovians could have ended up worse than the Province. I'm glad you helped us divert their mating drive to something more conventional. We showed them there is no liquid water anywhere on the other side of the rift, so their fight would not have lasted long. After a standoff, they agreed to be stationed here. They're working with the ESC and the Stozi empire now."

Paul turned to him and licked his nose. "I'm always here if you need to use me again."

"Ihara tells me you have over four hundred new profiles in your database."

"Just as many orders to fill."

"You might be the richest person in the galaxy. You could retire."

"I'm happy. It's like dreaming all the time. I never want it to stop."

Blunt smiled again. "Well, things should be a little quieter for a while. Enjoy your shore leave." He turned to go.

"Commander."

Blunt turned halfway to him. Paul rose and stood beside the bed. "You know there's only one male on this station who doesn't have a profile."

Blunt's smile changed to a grin. "It bothers you, doesn't it?"

"No, I just..." He looked at his feet, then up at the human again. "Would you like me to make one for you now? It would be no trouble."

"Thank you for the offer, but I don't need your services. Good night, Paul."

He turned and left. The door slid closed and locked behind him. Paul leaned on the bed, disappointed. Paul had been on this station for many years. People had told him the Atlins never wanted to deal with their own problems, and the Grovians were intimidating, and Jakoz were judgmental hypocrites, and Stozi were self-righteous, and Telosen were terrible at interpersonal interactions, and humans were always saying one thing while thinking another. Paul had never met an Atlin who didn't want to confront a problem, or felt intimidated by a Grovian, or saw any arrogance in a Jakoz, or heard anything self-righteous from a Stozi, or met any Telosen who lacked personal skills, or sensed anything two-faced about a human. He felt at ease with every single individual who had ever entered this room except for one.

Commander Blunt was the only person he didn't fully understand. The only person who made Paul feel uneasy. As he stood there staring at the curtain covering the locked door, he felt uncomfortable, and he wondered if it really did bother him.

And why.

5

INT – PAUL'S SHOP / 0730

High-pitched purring sounds roused Paul out of a dreamless sleep. He propped himself up on his hands and looked around. The bed was covered in furry, cube-shaped creatures varying in size from one of his paws to that of his head. Their fur ranged in color from bright reds to dull greens.

The floor was covered in them. Some were climbing the walls. Many of them were purring, which filled the room with a soft, adorable, droning noise.

Paul rose to all fours and looked for an empty place to put his foot down. There weren't many gaps between them on the bed, but Paul managed to spider-walk down to the floor.

His foot landed on one. It squealed. Paul raised his foot and looked down. The cube of orange fur resumed purring. Paul lowered his foot and nudged it out of the way. It hobbled a few centimeters to the left, and Paul slipped his foot into the gap. He swung his other leg over and found another gap on the floor.

Paul stood in the middle of an ocean of these purring creatures. In some areas they were sitting on top of one another. He looked around the room and noticed the plate covering the air vent on the far wall was gone. A furry creature fell from the vent and bounced soundlessly across the pile on the floor before coming to a rest among the brood.

Paul bent down and picked one up. It purred louder in his hand. He turned it over. Its underbelly was just as furry as its back. He could see no legs, mouth, or eyes, but he felt a heartbeat.

Paul was up to his knees in these things. They seemed harmless enough, and the white noise of their purring was pleasant. Still, he wondered what happened. He stepped high and pushed his foot between two cubes of fluff. He worked it all the way down to the floor, nudging several of them to the side. The creatures he touched purred louder as his leg brushed them. One step at a time, Paul crossed the room and stood at the door. Pulling the curtain aside, he peeked through the window.

The inner diamond was also covered in these little animals. Several ESC officers were collecting them in drums and crates and bags and anything else they could find. The bar appeared to be closed. Everyone seemed to be helping.

Paul had seen some strange things happen on Far Space 3, but this was one of the more amusing.

He heard poofing noises behind him, and he turned to see eight more animals rolling from the vents and then settling into the pile.

He turned back to the window and reached for the button that would open the door. His hand seized up. Paul wanted to know what these things were and where they came from. If the entire crew really was helping to collect them, he wanted to do his part.

His hand shook. All he had to do was push the button and open the door, but at the same time the thought of leaving made him sick to his stomach. Here was safety. Out there was wide-open spaces and uncertainty. He had been out there before, against his will, and only the kindness of strangers helped him find his way to someplace he could settle.

He withdrew his hand and backed away, wading through the animals. He stroked the warm cube of fluff in his arms as he trudged to the back of the room. He brushed a small pile of fur off his chair and sat. He wondered whom he should call about this. As he debated, twenty more animals fell from the vents and rolled to a rest, adding to the white noise of gentle purring.

This seemed like a call for the Fißeri. He pushed the com button.

"Systems Update Specialist Ihara."

A brief pause while the computer routed his request to the appropriate person. *Paul? Is that you?*

"Yes, my shop is being invaded by adorable animals. I can barely move in here."

Hang tight, Paul. I'll send someone over.

"Thank you."

The call ended. Paul waded through the animals and climbed onto the bed, still holding this rather large block of fluff. He sat in the middle of a pile of them. He reached around and gathered up a bunch. They all purred louder as he embraced them.

He felt proud of himself. He had just reached out to someone.

The collective noise of the creatures felt soothing. Paul closed his eyes and let himself slip away into a dreamlike state.

It occurred to him that if even Hadron's was closed, then all the shops on the inner diamond must be closed as well. Everyone was probably helping to collect these animals, and this meant he would have no clients today.

Paul opened his eyes. His heart raced. He thought about it. A whole day. A whole day...

Maybe longer.

He began to feel as if he were about to open the door and walk out again.

Since the moment he had gained consciousness, this was what he had done. Sex had been all he could think about every waking moment of those thirty-plus years. Now he faced the possibility of not doing it for a day or so.

If he wasn't having sex, then what would he do?

He looked at the door, rocking gently back and forth with his armful of animals. Another dozen of them fell from the vents and tumbled to a rest.

He could help them clean up. All he would have to do was emerge from his shop and start helping. He could ask where they came from and what was going on instead of wondering.

But what would he talk to them about? He didn't know how to help with cleanup, and even if someone told him where they came from, he would not understand most of what they said. Whenever someone told him things, so much of it made no sense to him. What would Paul say in reply? He had no childhood. No education. He had been created for one purpose, and if he wasn't doing that, then who was he?

He didn't want to step outside ever again. Beyond this room was the answer, and he had faced it once. Those born or hatched by natural means did not have to question their reason to exist. They knew their parents had created them, and they were now free to make their way in the universe the way their parents had. Paul, however, had been created to do something, and apart from that, the universe had no place for him.

He had felt as if the universe swept him up and took him for a ride. Here in this room, he was doing exactly what he had been created to do, and it made him happy.

Still, from time to time he looked out that window, and he wondered if he could be doing anything else. He wondered if he was even capable of learning. The one time he had been out there, during those terrifying years between the lab and this room, he had learned that he was not capable of doing anything else. His mind did not seem to have space to learn how to converse with people the way they expected, or retain knowledge, or comprehend anything. Ideas just didn't stick the way they seemed to with others. The Atlins had tried to teach him to play simple games, but Paul could never remember the rules no matter how many times he heard them.

He was a product of his genetic engineering, and he was happy doing what he did, but right now, alone with his thoughts, all he wanted to do was go out there and help somehow. The thought of leaving the room and discovering he would not even be able to do such a simple thing as clean up the rest of these animals kept him on the bed, cuddled up to these purring cubes of warm fluff.

Some time later, Paul heard the door chime.

"Unlock."

The computer recognized his voice and unbolted the door. He heard a few curse words as it slid shut.

"So this is where they've been hiding," Aaza Kas-sti said.

"The one place we didn't think to look." Ihara's voice. The black-skinned lizard had a belly. This was the longest Paul had seen him keep his clutch of eggs.

The sound of a communicator being activated. "Sela to Cylinder, we found another hiding place. It's Paul's shop."

Understood.

Paul turned to the door, still sitting under a pile of warm fur. A canine hand parted the curtain and trudged through the animals. Her touch made them purr louder.

"Paul! Glad to see you stayed above the flood."

Paul's tail wagged, hitting a few animals and making them coo. "What's happening?"

"Oh, that's right," Ihara said, the thin lizard high-stepping through the animals. "You probably just woke up."

Aaza was making her way to the vent. "Me, Ihara, Lawrence, Blunt, and Cylinder found the planet where these creatures came from."

Ihara was making his way to the other side of the room to the other open air vent. "Very weird place. We had a fantastic adventure trying to rescue them from extinction."

The Telose bird stood in the doorway, looking over the room. "I would have liked to meet Captain Kord. I hear he had a way with women."

Aaza had to raise her voice to be heard over all the purring she was stirring up. "Seems this planet is the center of a time travel conspiracy. Everyone either hates or adores these little creatures. We must have met a thousand people from fifty different time periods. Captain Kord was among them. The man's a legend in the ESC."

"He overthrew so many indigenous cultures in the name of democracy," Ihara said.

"Such a role model," Sela's eyes widened in a smile. "Glad we could prevent his assassination and save these creatures."

Paul heard. He listened. He tried to force himself to understand, but he did not know what an assassination was, or what it meant to go back in time. "These things?"

Aaza had found the vent cover and was now putting it back up, using a laser gun to melt the metal in place. "They're called *hiddles*. Lawrence very heterosexually tells us they're multiversally existent. Each one lives in several parallel universes at once. Enough food and heat and it pulls its counterpart from other quantum realities, then that pulls another from a different reality, and so on."

Ihara was also melting the vent cover in place on his side. "It's a unique method of reproduction. Deserves to be preserved and studied. We brought a few back with us.

Guess they found the station favorable. Lots of recursions of hiddles from other universes are pooling here. They got a little out of hand. The station is shut down until we can collect them all."

Sela was smiling at Paul with her eyes. "Looks like they found a nice place to hide. We'll take them to a new home as soon as we corral them."

Paul's tail beat another group of hiddles. "Thank you. Um, how long will the station be closed?"

Ihara was now walking toward the bed Paul was sitting on. "We hope to have things back up by this time tomorrow. Could be longer, depending on how fast we find all their hiding places."

Aaza was also walking up to his bed. "You get a day off, Paul. You could help us clean up if you like. Would be a nice break in the routine."

Paul shivered. He considered it. He convulsed harder. Going outside... Did he want to try again? The last time he had tried had only confirmed his fear, and this time he would have it confirmed again in front of people who knew him and liked him.

"I'm happy here," he said at last. "I think I just want to sleep."

Aaza smiled. "I'm disappointed, too. I only have two more chapters to read in my book, but my table is buried. Reading just isn't the same in Hadron's. We're sealing the airways so they can't get in. A team will be here to clean them up. They'll also go through the vents and fish the rest out."

Ihara had climbed on top of Paul's bed and was melting the overhead vent cover to the frame.

"That'll do it. Temporary fix." He climbed down and leaned on the bed, facing the scaliefox. "We saw something interesting on Kord's ship."

Paul felt the mattress depressing on the other side as Aaza leaned on it. Paul turned to face her.

"Someone who looked a lot like you, Paul."

Paul sat up straight, squeezing his bouquet of hiddles tighter. "A... Another...?"

"That's right," Ihara answered. Paul faced him now. "Another half lizard half canine. All scales in the front, all fur in the back. But she had black fur and red scales."

"We were wondering if you had any relatives."

Paul turned to her. He opened his mouth. He almost said it. He almost told her about— He began to shake. He huddled into himself. He then lay under the pile of hiddles.

He felt a lizard hand on his shoulder. "She had the same reaction when we asked her about you."

Paul didn't know when they left. He didn't know how long he lay there shivering, but when he stopped, the door was closed, and all the hiddles were gone. He heard sounds in the vents. People talking and a lot of purring.

He stood up and checked the machine. No orders pending, and he wished for another armada of Grovians to mount him one after the other, never letting him rest. Instead, he had the day to himself. He could think of nothing he wanted to do.

He decided to take a tiny chance. He walked back to the desk and sat down at the terminal.

"Computer, display information relating to Captain Kord."

Paul saw an image of an ESC vessel, but it seemed strange in appearance, more like a toy than a real spaceship. He read. Nothing made sense. He asked the computer to read the text to him, and he listened as he scrolled the text while the computer highlighted it in time with the synthetic voice. He forgot everything he heard within seconds. All he could think about was why there were no images of Captain Kord without clothes and why there was no information about what his penis looked like. His mind drifted to how it might differ from the usual human template, and how it would feel under his tail, and if he would be just as good at romancing Paul as he must have been at romancing women. He closed the page and walked back to the bed, shaking again.

An entire day.

INT – PAUL'S SHOP / 1340

Paul woke up to the sound of the door being forced open. Someone on the inner diamond was heaving it aside a few centimeters at a time. Paul noticed the lights were off, and the door panel was also dark. He propped himself up and looked at the desk. The terminal was blank. The printer in the back was still on. Paul sat cross-legged on the bed and faced whoever was coming, making sure his legs formed a nest for his loins.

Finally open, the people stepped aside, and through the curtain walked an Atlin Paul never thought he would see again.

"U'kar!" Paul bounced.

The hairless feline wearing a uniform as angular as the station stood at the entrance and spread his arms. "*Pwaal!* It is so good to be back." He crossed the room and embraced the scaliefox. "I knew I'd find you here!"

"I'm here. Still happy."

U'kar laughed and released him. "Business doing well, I presume."

"Yes, and you were the only one who kept ordering sleeves to be sent to Atlina Prime."

"At great personal expense, but worth it if it helped keep you in business."

"I always liked your profile."

The feline smiled wider. "If anyone else had said that I'd assume they were flattering me, but I know you too well." He began strolling around the room. "I see you got some new furniture. And the air vent covers are... melted in place? Something wrong with them?"

"We had a Hiddle invasion a few months ago."

"Ah, yes, I heard about that. Very amusing. Wish I could have seen it myself."

Paul lifted himself and turned to keep facing him as he walked about the room.

"It has been seven years since I was in charge of running this station. Then the Atlin government decided to end our customer support operations here, and we turned the only remaining station over to the ESC. I remember telling Adrian about you. It was the last thing I mentioned before I left the station. I told him to have pity on you and let you do your thing, as you couldn't survive outside this room. I'm relieved to see he listened. Forgive me if I have a glimmer of nostalgia in my eye. It's just that of all the parts of Far Space 3, I wanted to see this place again the most. You keep it clean for the work you do."

Paul's tail wagged. The Atlin smiled at Paul.

"I remember when you first arrived. A freighter crew dumped you here, and we weren't sure if you were sentient or not. You were incoherent, but one of my doctors took pity on you and nursed you back to health. Finally you were able to talk, but all you wanted to do was suck off members of my medical team."

Paul winced thinking about those days. "I remember."

"Naturally when I heard about this, I had to come down to see this specimen in person, and the rumors were true. You were very good with your tongue, and you enticed everyone to mount you. You were insatiable. Some of those men might have just kept you in the lab and used you, but one of my maintenance engineers had an idea for how we could give you a life. I liked his proposal, so I assigned a few people to his team, and they gave you this vacant shop."

"They taught me how to use the machine. What money was. It was so long ago."

"Not nearly as long as it feels, and they did more than teach you how to use it. They practically invented it for you."

U'kar stopped by the desk. He touched it in a few places and shook his head.

"Seems Adrian wiped out the systems here, too."

Paul's tail wagged and he turned to the printer. "Not my machine."

"Yes, I remember it was never integrated into the mainframe. You didn't lose your database. That's just the good news I needed to brighten my day. I suppose you're wondering what I'm doing here."

"Has the Fluidic Province come?"

"Oh my, you are so far behind, but I don't mind bringing you up to speed. Months ago I forged an alliance between the Atlin Empire and the Fluidic Province. They've been sending Setjalar ships through the rift and into our borders, amassing forces on all our worlds, preparing for the inevitable. The Province has already begun moving in. Atlina Prime is complying with their demands."

"Oh. I was wondering when the Fluidic Province would arrive."

U'kar approached the bed. "That day has come at last."

"So what do they want? Why are they coming?"

"That's an odd thing. I hope someone at least told you the Life is Fluidic."

Paul nodded.

"Good, you're not so far behind then. We have spoken with the Life frequently over the last few years. Seems in their universe, creatures did not evolve in water. Their plants and animals are not water-based. In fact, water itself is alive over there. Naturally when they saw what's in this universe, all those vast oceans and lakes and rivers, they assumed the water just needed the right stimulus and it would all congeal and wake up. Just imagine the oceans on Atlina Prime condensing into a few billion creatures like Cylinder. Well this is what they've been doing wherever that rift opens up. They send the Setjalar in to keep the water-based life forms in place while they try to raise the oceans. It's absurd, frankly, but who are we to stop them? Defeat is inevitable, so why not ally with them? In exchange for our cooperation, the Life will allow Atlina Prime exclusive rights to travel between the worlds and sell our goods to all the other water-based species. With everyone in the universe confined to their own world while the Life tries to bring water to sentience, they will need things. We can provide those things. Even the Life sees the benefit of this arrangement. The real goal, of course, is to discontinue our customer service support network. Being the sole provider of goods and services for the Universe of Dead Water means no need to put a good face on it. No need to have a return policy. No need to search for another species to be the face of our problems."

None of this made sense to Paul.

U'kar smirked. "I can tell when I've lost you, but I don't hold it against you, Number Twenty-three. Do you still prefer *pwaal*?"

Paul nodded.

U'kar smiled. "I always felt bad about your name. My medical team started calling you that. I never found out if it was a term of endearment or if they were being condescending. I thought you deserved better, but it seems to have carried over to the human languages as well. Paul. I give you my personal guarantee as both new commander of this station *and* as the Atlin liaison to the Fluidic Province that you are in no danger." He stopped at the bed and loomed over Paul. "This room will remain yours, and you may remain here, doing what you do, on one condition. That once we get the doors working again, I will have my own access code, and I will have the right—no, the privilege of your ass anytime I may desire."

"That sounds good."

He placed a hand on Paul's muzzle and felt it. Paul closed his eyes. He hadn't been touched in hours and it made him hard. He felt a hand encircle it and give it a squeeze.

"Just like the old days," U'kar continued. "I expect little will change from how the ESC ran this station. The only real difference is that soon this will be the nerve center of the war. No more running a Customer Support Station. Soon I will get to look our customers in the eye and tell them... *No.* Such a simple thing. Such a wonderful thing. So much meaning contained in that single word. Every Atlin everywhere will be able to say it to anyone they please. No need to put a face on it. No need to hire out our support network. Thanks to me, we will be seen as a decisive people who stand firm in their beliefs. No more hiding behind representatives and letting them bear the burden. Just us. The Atlin race will forever be known for its firmness because now there will be nothing to stop us from saying no to everyone. Remembering you and your plight keeps me grounded in reality. Never let it be said that I am unwilling to deal with problems."

"Thank you."

U'kar crossed the room and gestured to the door. "We won't be able to close the door until systems are restored, but I will assign a guard." He paused at the door, turned and smirked. "Feel free to have a drink at Hadron's. He's still here—oh, that's right. You're not alone. Z-rank Sela is here, too. Typical Telosen. Even as they rebel against us, they never forget their training. I can respect that. I look forward to working with all of you."

U'kar walked through the curtain and rounded the corner. Paul shuddered. He had hoped to feel him under his tail again. He wondered if he would get any clients today with systems being wiped out.

Paul heard a few orders ping. He slid off the bed and walked to the back. The terminal was still on and responding, and his database of profiles was indeed intact. This order was from U'kar, a request for reprints of fourteen Atlin profiles. Paul guessed they were back on the station, and he should be ready. He nearly finished at just the thought of meeting all these people again.

EXT – FARS3 SURROUNDED BY ATLIN AND SETJALAR VESSELS

INT – PAUL'S SHOP / 1016

This Atlin stopped thrusting. Paul felt him pulsing against his ring. He patted Paul on the shoulder as he finished.

"I forgot how much fun this was," he said.

Paul looked back at him, panting. "I've missed feeling Atlin in me."

He rubbed Paul's rear and squeezed it. Then he pulled out and stepped aside. The next Atlin in line made sure his sleeve was on, and then he pushed in. Paul leaned forward and buried his head in his arms as he started to thrust.

"I'm glad U'kar is letting you stay," someone behind Paul said. "I was worried the Province would consider you a security risk. Guess the commander likes you too much."

"Paul a security risk? He never leaves this room. U'kar knows that. Besides, how can you not like the little thing?

Brain hardwired to comprehend cock and only that. We're helping him more than he's helping us."

Everyone laughed. Paul wagged his tail. He shuddered as the stimulating nubs on his head rubbed against him.

Paul looked up at the far wall. Four Setjalar stood by the door, holding rifles. They had been there for hours, and Paul had begun to wonder if U'kar really had sent them. It had been days since the Fluidic Province had taken over the station, and since the computer systems had been restored, the Setjalar had been guarding the door from the inside. Different guards every hour or so. They never said anything, even when Paul tried to talk to them. They just watched.

The last three clients of the day used Paul. They had already ordered and paid for their sleeves, so Paul did not have to do anything else. When they left, Paul expected the Setjalar guards to follow them out and stand by the door, even though the lock worked again.

This time the three guards did not move. Paul lay on his stomach and observed them. Minutes later, someone rang the door chime. One of the guards pushed the button. The curtain parted, and Lak'la'ta'an entered the room.

Paul's ears perked. The three guards set their weapons by the door. Lak'la'ta'an marched up to the bed just as Paul slid off it. Paul embraced the feathered canine, who returned the embrace but otherwise remained rigid.

"Paul... it has been a confusing time since I met you."

"So much has happened. I don't hear very much about it." The other three guards had surrounded them. Paul looked at each one in turn. "What's happening?"

"I am still Second. This is my First and my Third. I showed them what you showed me. Seems your prototype of me also fits them."

"It does?"

"The sleeves you made fit every Setjalar we tried them on."

Paul's tail wagged.

The feathery dog on Paul's left spoke up next. "I am Do'loth, First rank of our unit. Lak'la'ta'an took a great risk showing me. Had I not been intrigued, I would have had him terminated."

"Zo'moreth, Third rank. Our entire unit explored these sensations you showed us, however when we tried to alert higher command of what we were doing, we were told to cease immediately."

Lak'la'ta'an spoke next. "The three of us tried to forget and return to our duties as normal, but we came to the mutual agreement that we did not want to forget. We continued in secret. We showed a few others about the hidden organ inside their slits. Some were intrigued. Others feared this would be a distraction on the battlefield."

Paul was hard just being so close to them. "Was it?"

"It proved to be, in some cases." Lak'la'ta'an answered. "When our unit had to work with others, some noted our performance was decreased. We blamed it on tainted nutrient solution. The whole time though, we were finding new ways to stimulate one another, especially after a successful battle. Always in secret, away from other soldiers."

Do'loth and Zo'moreth began unclipping their armor plating. Paul's tail rose, and he worked a finger under Lak'la'ta'an's chest plate. The canine removed it, and Paul knelt facing them. Their bodies were hard but their feathers were soft. He wondered why everyone feared the Setjalar.

The next thing Paul remembered was being mounted one after the other. They kept this up on a rotational basis, two resting, one mounting. By the time he was finished, one of the other two would be ready to go.

Paul remained in that dreamlike state all night. It reminded him of days long since past. Before FarS3. Before the Atlins ended his wandering at the mercy of the whims of the galaxy. Those wonderful days of his youth when this feeling lasted entire years and nothing else existed.

EXT – FARS3, MERCHANT SHIPS NOW AMONG THE ATLIN AND SETJALAR VESSELS

INT – PAUL'S SHOP / 0620

Paul opened his eyes. He was still in bed next to Do'loth. It was a rare and wonderful thing when Paul met people he wanted to feel inside him without a sleeve, and Paul had taken all three of them one after the other, felt their heat, even confirmed that the fingerprint-like pattern on their organs was indeed identical.

At least one of them had stayed with Paul every night for the past week. Sometimes all three managed to stay, and Paul was glad for the company. He often woke up in the middle of night with a penis inside him, and he felt content in a way he hadn't felt since he first opened this shop.

Do'loth rose from the bed and strapped his armor on. Paul rolled to his back and reached out. Do'loth leaned over and felt the scales on Paul's chest, then ran his hand around the back of his neck and felt where scales changed to fur. Paul wrapped his arms around him. He leaned closer.

The three Setjalar seemed to grasp the appeal of being close like this. Paul wondered if it was affection. He wondered if creatures designed to be soldiers were capable of feeling it.

His companion for the night slipped the rest of his armor on, picked up his weapon, and left the room. Paul stretched. He walked to the side room and used the lavatory.

He then checked the machine for orders. Only three today, but business had been slow since the Fluidic Province had arrived. He hadn't seen Sela or Hadron. As far as Paul knew, nothing had changed except he very much enjoyed spending his nights with the Setjalar. It felt so strange experiencing the same profile on three different individuals.

They each had their own personality, though whenever they tried to speak to Paul, it was always about battles and war and conquest. Zo'moreth tried telling Paul about how he managed a laser shot to the head of an ESC officer from two kilometers away, but it didn't make much sense to Paul. He didn't know what a kilometer was, or why it was so impressive to kill someone from that distance, or even why that someone needed to be killed.

Paul tried talking to them about his experiences, but they seemed completely ignorant of the appeal of scent and feeling and desire. Their lives meant nothing to one another, and neither seemed capable of bridging that gap. All they knew was they liked how this made them feel, they wanted more of it, and they knew Paul was eager to help.

He switched on the external sign and set the printer to run the two orders he had received overnight. Paul felt empty again. He didn't like this feeling. He went to the desk and sat down.

Minutes later, the door chimed. Paul pressed the button and let him in, already wagging his tail and peeking from his sheath in anticipation of a new profile to make. A Setjalar walked in, sidearm holstered. Paul did not recognize him.

"Yes?" he asked.

The canine's feathers ruffled. "Lak'la'ta'an sent me. He told me to try something the other day, which I did, and now I am confused. I was told you knew how to help."

Paul's tail wagged as he stood up and crossed the room. "What did he tell you to do?"

He remained upright, still in military attention. "To remove the piece of armor from between my legs and touch myself where the plate had covered my body. I had never had a reason to remove my armor before, but it sounded intriguing. I am not sure what I felt."

"I can show you what to do with it."

Stone-faced, he began unbuckling the codpiece.

"What is your name?"

"I would rather not give my name and rank."

"I understand."

The piece of armor fell away, revealing his slit. Paul felt it with a finger. The soldier remained steadfast and statuesque while his organ slipped out. Paul gripped it, teasing the spongy, labyrinthine ridges all the way around. His knot hadn't swelled yet, so Paul took the chance to wrap both hands around it. He felt up and down a few times, room for two more of Paul's hands so plenty of space to move. It was so slick fluid accumulated between Paul's fingers and dripped on the carpet.

The soldier hadn't reacted. Paul slid a finger down the underside of the shaft and into his slit.

Now the soldier shuddered, and Paul licked his lips. He leaned against the soldier's leg, letting his cock rest on his shoulder.

"These are intriguing sensations. I do not understand why my body has them."

"I can show you that, too," Paul said, nuzzling his organ.

"I would be grateful. Proceed."

Paul kept a few stacks of Setjalar sleeves around the room in case this happened. He grabbed one, rolled the sleeve over it. Watching the sleeve match the peaks and valleys of the fingerprint pattern that covered this organ gave

Paul a prickle of pride at the work he did. He lubed it up with the slick on his paws.

As with Lak'la'ta'an the first time Paul met him, this soldier didn't know what to do next. Figuring he would not enjoy the bed, Paul nudged him to lie down on the floor. The soldier did so with rigidity, as if trying to remain in formation. Paul climbed over his chest and sat down on the soldier easily, taking him to the hilt in one motion.

Suddenly the solider became alive, as if for the first time. His hips began working, and now he began feeling Paul up and down. Paul saw a change in his face, and indeed his entire posture. No longer a soldier, something else had taken over, and now he was thrusting Paul as the scaliefox braced himself on pectoral muscles twice the size of Paul's head.

Some naive clients went too rough. Others leaned more toward the gentle side, not sure how much Paul could handle. This soldier had clearly been gripped by a new feeling, and he craved more of it. He rolled Paul over to his back and took control.

Paul lay splayed out on the floor, legs up, pinned under a male three times his size. The soldier had discovered he could get more of this feeling in this way, and he took advantage of it. Paul closed his eyes and let himself slip into a dream where only this feeling existed and he never had to think about anything else.

When Paul came out of it, the soldier had pinned his arms down and he was practically lying on Paul. The Construct took the chance to lick the soldier's muzzle. Feathers felt strange on the tongue, and to see them on a canine body was equally surprising.

When he pulled out, Paul felt empty, and he turned to look at the soldier. "Are you all right?"

The soldier was looking down at himself, completely mystified by what his body had just done. It was still jutting from between his legs, still throbbing, though nothing was coming out anymore. Paul sat up and gripped the base of the sleeve. He worked it off and set it on the edge of the bed.

"That was," the soldier began, as if trying to remember how to be a soldier again. "Interesting."

"Don't tell too many people about it. I hear if the Life found out you were doing this, they might discipline you."

"I understand. You have my gratitude for your assistance."

He attached the codpiece again, and then walked out the door. Paul stretched and waited for the next client.

INT – PAUL'S SHOP / 1850

Paul was beginning to think something strange was going on. He was running off all these copies of the Setjalar profile, and somebody was paying for them. Funds were coming from multiple accounts, but they weren't clients. Paul needed to purchase polymer material from time to time, but he found to his surprise that someone was buying it for him and having it delivered and installed into the printer.

He was grateful for the assistance, as he'd been seeing a lot of Setjalar in here lately. He'd lost count of how many had come through this week, but he had seen at least fifty of them in the last three days, all had heard of something interesting their bodies could do. Today alone he had shown eight soldiers exactly what their bodies could do.

It still amazed Paul that the same profile fit every single one of them. He was starting to get bored of the same thing inside him again and again, but each individual had a unique way of using it, and they all had different scents and voices, so Paul still had some variety to keep himself interested.

By the end of the day, Paul lay on the bed and stretched out on his stomach. This had been a fascinating change since the Fluidic Province took over.

The door chimed. Paul used a voice command to let them in. Lak'la'ta'an strolled through the curtain, and Paul sat upright, tail wagging. Lak'la'ta'an let the door lock. The inner diamond was closed now save for the night crew at Hadron's.

Lak'la'ta'an was removing his armor. Paul liked it when he did this. It wasn't easy for him, given his bulk and how his muscles collided even before doing something strenuous with them. Removing the one chest plate also meant his vial had nowhere to hang, so it dangled freely from the tube that ran into his shoulder. He climbed into bed with Paul and wrapped his feathery arms around him. Paul practically disappeared, being surrounded by Setjalar muscle. He pushed his hips back into Lak'la'ta'an's, hoping to feel him inside.

"Lak'la'ta'an, I'm curious. You're bred to be a soldier. You said your body was designed to use the vials for all nutrients. You never have to eat or drink or use the lavatory. What did they do to your mind when they made you?"

"You'll have to clarify."

"I mean... Are you capable of thinking of things that aren't military? Do you understand what this is?"

He didn't answer for a long time. He kept feeling the border where Paul's scales became fur.

"It has been very difficult to understand you. I keep attempting to, but so little of your life makes sense to me."

"Almost nothing the Setjalar tell me makes sense. I'm not even sure I understand what a war is. People have tried to explain it to me, but as soon as I hear it, it slides away."

"I believe I can understand what you experience in some ways. This drive to be close to someone."

"We're both Constructs. Our bodies and minds were designed for one purpose. Does that mean we can't do anything else? If you wanted to, could you be something other than a soldier?"

"Not without the vials."

"Doctor Dorset heterosexually told me a while ago the ESC hasn't figured out how to make them. If they do... would you be able to do something else?"

"What else is there besides combat? This is a fascinating new feeling, but I would not be happy living only for it."

"There's a whole universe out there, and I'm not in it."

Lak'la'ta'an held him tighter. Paul liked the contrast of soft feathers covering unyielding muscle.

"Lak'la'ta'an, sometime will you... Will you help me leave this room for a while?"

The Setjalar held his breath. His hand fell still. "Are you afraid to leave?"

"Very. Do you understand what fear is?"

"I was trained it is how lesser creatures preserved their own lives. Caution in battle taken to an extreme that paralyzes the mind. What do you fear?"

"I am afraid of what I am."

He reached down and felt his rear. Moments later, Paul felt something hot and slick sliding under his tail. Paul felt so much better now.

"I believe I understand this," Lak'la'ta'an said, thrusting Paul a few times. "I enjoy being close to you, and I desire to help you as one solider helps another during combat."

Paul wasn't sure what this meant to Lak'la'ta'an, or the other soldiers. Paul wondered if he ever would understand exactly what they were getting out of this.

EXT – ESC AND GROVIAN VESSELS AT HY-PER, APPROACHING FARS3

INT – PAUL'S SHOP / 1740

An alarm was going off, and the overhead computer voice was telling all Province personnel to evacuate the station. Paul leaped to his feet and looked around. He ran to the desk and tried to pull up more information, but the systems were locked. He leaned on the desk, not sure what to do. He didn't even know what day it was.

Minutes later, Paul's door chimed, and he pushed the button to open it. Lak'la'ta'an ran through, holding a rifle at ready. Paul's tail hid between his legs. It did not cover his sheath or his testicles.

"It's time to leave," said the soldier. "The ESC is retaking the station. They broke through our lines. We can't remain."

"I... I'm not Province."

"If you want to accompany us, you will be welcomed by a good many Setjalar."

"What would I do out there? This is all I can do! I'm not a soldier! They won't let me go with you or anyone... It —it would be easier if you stayed here."

Lak'la'ta'an gradually fell out of his military stance. He looked around, and for the first time, he seemed open to a possibility he had never considered.

"What would I do here? I'm a soldier. My senses are designed for that. I would be looked upon with suspicion, assuming someone can synthesize vials for me."

Someone peeked through the door. "Lak'la'ta'an, it's last call. The shuttles are leaving. The fleet is almost here."

"We can find a place for you."

"We'll find a place for you."

Paul and Lak'la'ta'an had spoken at the same time. Their eyes locked. Neither breathed.

The Setjalar approached him and stood at his side.

"You are too afraid to leave this room. I will make a soldier out of you here."

Paul's tail wagged and he held him around his waist.

They stood as the alarm sounded and the computer warned that shuttles were departing in one minute. Lak'la'ta'an held Paul around his back. A few seconds later, the alarm stopped. Lak'la'ta'an began leading Paul to the door. Paul's heart raced. He considered becoming a soldier. He considered being able to shoot someone from a kilometer away with a weapon not designed for that. Could his enhanced senses be used for that instead of sex?

He let himself believe it. He was happy in his room with people inside him all day, but lately he felt he was in his room out of fear, not out of joy for what he did, and he wanted this barrier to drop. He held Lak'la'ta'an tighter around his back.

"You will have to tell them I'm here. I'll be shot on sight."

Paul faced the door. "I can do that. I *will* do that."

He worked a hand under the armor and gave Lak'la'ta'an's abs one last rub before walking to the door, the canine's feathery hand falling away behind him. Paul began to shiver, but this time he wouldn't back down. Lak'la'ta'an valued combat, and he was determined to prove he could live up to that.

Paul was ten steps from the door. He heard a conversion beam behind him and turned. A Grovian was teleporting into the room. Lak'la'ta'an heard it and spun around, raising his weapon.

The beam ended, and Lak'la'ta'an fired his weapon, scoring a direct hit on the Grovian's chest, boring a small hole in it. The saurian fell to the ground and fired back.

The laser struck Lak'la'ta'an on the face. His head exploded, and his body slumped over. Paul stared as he dropped to his knees.

"It's all right, Paul," said the Grovian. "You're safe now."

Paul recognized the voice, and he pictured this reptile's ridged organ in his mind's eye. He knew exactly which profile was gres and where it was in the database and even when je last purchased sleeves and how much je had spent in total since je had been stationed at FarS3.

"He was joining us! He was going to be with me! I wanted to help him be..."

"Oh, Paul." The Grovian was rolling to gres feet, bleeding and unable to move one arm. "He still had his weapon. He was hoping you'd call Commander Blunt and he'd use the chance to kill him. A way to give his life purpose before he died."

Paul's ears sagged.

The saurian stumbled past him, patting him on the head. "I am relieved you're safe. Well done. This battle will be commemorated in song, and your name will be in the refrain."

Je walked out the door. Paul stared at the headless body on the floor. He heard more footsteps behind him, on the inner diamond.

Paul considered the reptile's words. If Lak'la'ta'an had simply seen an opportunity to make a kill, then it proved the Setjalar were incapable of being anything but soldiers loyal to the Fluidic Province, even to the death.

But if Lak'la'ta'an were telling the truth, and he really did intend to stay on FarS3 for Paul's sake, then that meant he had stepped out of his own room, and his reward had been death—the only reward that awaited Paul as well.

Paul knelt alone for some time, staring at the corpse and inhaling the smell of blood.

He heard footsteps coming up behind him and felt a hand on his shoulder. He recognized the scent of Commander Blunt.

"You did well, Paul. Thank you for your help."

"What?"

"Z-rank Sela and Hadron noticed the Setjalar were interested in you. Hadron quietly paid and organized delivery for your supplies, and Sela sent people to you and made sure the Atlins didn't notice. They figured once the Setjalar got a taste of this new feeling, they would neglect their regular duties, and sure enough, their patrol ships stopped moving for hours at a time. The number of ships decreased. Sometimes they were slow to return fire. Their hearts didn't seem to be into fighting anymore. We broke through their lines easily. Thanks to you, we retook the station in less than a month, and Sela and Hadron resolved their old grudges. Too bad you didn't see any of it. I would have liked to know how they managed to tolerate one another long enough to cooperate."

Paul sighed. "Glad to help... in the only way I can."

He patted Paul's shoulder. "You're a valuable member of my crew. Never forget that."

He turned to leave.

"If I had left to join the Province," Paul began, "and be with Lak'la'ta'an, what do you think would have happened to me?"

Blunt paused at the door, turning to Paul. "From what I know of the Setjalar, they would have left you behind as soon as you slowed them down."

"Even if they liked me?"

"It's war, Paul. You have a lot to learn."

"I don't think I can learn. I want to, but I can't."

"That's up to you. Everyone has a choice."

"Normal people do. He was created to be a soldier. What if he didn't have a choice? What if I don't either?"

Before Commander Blunt could answer, a voice came from his communicator.

Kas-sti to Blunt.

"Go ahead," said the commander.

Come to the command deck. U'kar is still here. I think he's delirious.

Paul heard U'kar screaming about the value of the word *no.* How he wanted to tell everyone *no, no, no, no, they can't exchange that no they can't have a discount what they see is what they get they should thank the Atlin race for all of it.*

"On my way."

Blunt practically sprinted out of Paul's shop. The door remained open. Paul climbed back onto the bed and forced himself to look at the body on the floor. Both possibilities seemed true. He sat in place while hundreds of Grovians and ESC jumped about on the inner diamond, celebrating victory.

7

INT – PAUL'S SHOP / 0213

The override chime on his lock woke Paul up. He raised his torso off the bed and stared at the door.

The door then chimed normally, twice.

Paul rose and sat upright on the bed, facing the door.

"Computer, raise the lights."

The room brightened to its usual level.

"Cylinder, is that you?"

No, Paul.

Commander Blunt's voice, at oh-two hundred hours.

"Come in."

The door slid to the side, and the commander parted the curtain and stepped into the room. He looked as if he had not slept or changed clothes in days.

"Is something wrong, commander?"

"Yes. Something is very wrong, and I need to talk about it."

Blunt walked to the Grovian chair and sat in the middle seat, legs wide, head between his hands, looking at the floor. Paul turned around on the bed and faced him.

"It's been two weeks since it happened. I can't talk to anyone about this. No one can know. Do you understand, Paul? You're the closest thing this station has to a counselor, and I know you won't tell anyone."

"No, I won't tell anyone. I might even forget it after you say it."

"Good. The war has been going badly for the Dead Water Alliance. That's what the media are calling it. It's supposed to be a term of endearment, describing our universe with nonliving water as a positive thing, but I can't bring myself to call it that. It's the Democratic Earth & Space Command Committed to Peace and Democracy, the Stozi Empire, and the Grovian Empire against the Fluidic Province and the Atlin Empire. They breed warriors who have no concern for their own lives. Their ships can outrun and outgun ours. They have every tactical advantage against us. And there's something else. Have you heard what the Life wants from our universe, Paul?"

"U'kar told me they want to bring the oceans to life."

"That's right. The Fluidics believe the oceans in our universe are merely dormant versions of themselves. Given the right stimulation, water will become sentient, and they want to push us aside to make it happen. A few weeks ago, I received a call from Command. They wanted me and Riack to go on a covert mission into Stozi territory. There were rumors the Province had quietly occupied a planet there, and we were to investigate."

Paul's tail wagged. The mention of his name brought the shape and pattern of Riack's profile to the foreground of his mind. "He has five spurs on his tip, plus an extra one on his shaft, each one triangular in shape. He told me they were filed that way as punishment for breaking too many return policy rules."

Blunt looked up at him, half smiling. "You always remember the important details. Yes, Riack. They wanted him because he is not a member of the ESC, so he is not bound by our moral code. Plus he has customer service experience, so he wouldn't be afraid to use deadly force without prejudice."

Blunt leaned back in the chair and unzipped his uniform top. "Stozi territory is still friendly, but we had to treat every person we met as a potential hostile. All of this was happening in secret. We met several Stozi who seemed sympathetic to the Life's cause. We had no choice. We had to kill them and take their ships. We must have switched vessels six times."

Blunt continued by relating how their journey into what should have been friendly territory turned into a perilous mission fraught with betrayal and murder. Command had not mentioned that the Stozi in this region seemed on the verge of defecting to the Province. Blunt and Riack had not anticipated having to treat the quadrupeds as their enemy.

Paul listened. He could remember every penis that had been inside him over the last two weeks. Paul even matched up the time Commander Blunt did this or that to what had been inside him at the time. It was the only way events outside this room made any sense.

Finally they reached their destination. They had to wear artificial scent generators and smear themselves with scent-neutralizing gel to mask their presence. That's when they saw the Life.

"The reconnaissance had been true. The Life was here. Hundreds of people just like Cylinder at the shore. Living puddles of water. They were in the ocean, on it, all around. Riack and I tried not to laugh. We gathered evidence, documented everything, including the Stozi we saw. Weeks we remained in hiding. And then... it happened. The unthinkable—the *impossible* happened!"

Paul didn't like hearing him angry. He wasn't used to this kind of distressed scent. Paul climbed down from the bed and jogged across the carpet. He sat next to the commander and leaned against him. Blunt leaned back in the chair and draped his arm behind Paul.

"The ocean began to congeal. It came to life, Paul. Living blobs of water. From horizon to horizon. Paul... It was beautiful. Even Riack was moved to tears. We had to hold on to one another other to keep the other quiet."

Commander Blunt was crying and sweating, but his scent was still terrified and distressed—not the usual reason humans in here perspired. Paul did not like the scent. He rubbed Blunt's chest through his uniform. It did not seem to help. Blunt fell silent for a minute, and then finally he resumed.

"Paul, nobody else can know this. What I'm about to tell you can't leave this room. Do you understand?"

Blunt was feeling Paul's shoulder. His scales, not his fur. Paul was nuzzling his neck, looking down at his pants, wondering more than ever what was under them.

"I understand."

"Paul, this means the Life is right. Our oceans... Our lakes. Every molecule of water in our universe could be alive. This must be what happened to Cylinder. It assumed it was sent from the other universe as a spy, but this shows that it comes from our universe. Our water is not dead. It just needs the right stimulation, and all of it will wake up. Something happened to the molecules in Cylinder, and it came to life by accident. That could happen to every molecule of water in our universe. It is possible."

"Well, that's good. Isn't it?"

"No, Paul, this is not good. If the Province is allowed to do this, it will mean there will be no water in the universe. Life here will cease to exist. The Life believes liquid life forms are the only true form of life. The rest of us are alive at water's expense. On that planet in Stozi territory, Riack and I deployed an experimental weapon. An anti-hydrogen bomb. AHaB, Command calls it. It prevents hydrogen and oxygen from bonding. After we documented what we saw, we lifted into orbit and set it off. We wiped them out. Not just the ocean. Everything on the hemisphere. Water will not be able to form there for at least eight hundred years. We had to do it. Paul, we had to. The fate of all we know in this universe depends on it. I keep telling myself I did the right thing. But... I believe I may have committed an unforgivable sin." Blunt pulled Paul closer. "We can't use this weapon, even as a last resort. There must be another way. We can talk to the Life. We can convince them it doesn't have to be this way, and yet I wonder if the Province is right. Is Fluidic life normal, and we are the exception? Do the oceans deserve a chance? What if... What if it should happen? Is our cause just? We are fighting for the right to exist at water's expense. That's noble. It's the right thing to do. It must be."

Paul licked behind Blunt's ear. Many humans had a stimulating spot behind one of their ears, and he wondered if Commander Blunt had one as well.

"Did any of this make sense to you, Paul?"

Paul stopped licking. He was glad Blunt's scent was calming down. "Some of it. I... I'm afraid I don't understand. Why is the Province fighting us? Why are we fighting them? Why can't we all just be in bed together?"

Blunt smiled as he leaned back in the chair. He giggled. The giggle became a laugh. The laugh rose in volume until he leaned forward and doubled over, crying, unable to breathe. He did this for about five minutes, and then he sat back and pulled Paul into an embrace.

"You're right, Paul. You're right."

Paul whimpered. He picked up Blunt's hand and moved it down to his sheath. The commander raised it and held it at his back.

"No, Paul, I'm not here for that. I just needed to tell someone. Oh, Paul, people like you need to be protected. In your room, everything works the way it should. All species get along, everyone makes love, and nobody fights over anything. I wish things outside worked that way. I would sell my soul to whatever deity could make that happen if it meant we could live in that galaxy. Perhaps I did sell my soul to make it happen. Or at least prevent our universe from becoming hell. I can live with that. If my soul is what it takes, then I will live with it."

Paul didn't know what to say. Usually when someone touched his sheath or balls, he knew exactly what would happen next. Some clients were nervous, so letting them touch him gave them permission.

INT – PAUL'S SHOP / 0400

Movement woke Paul, and he sat up on the bed. Blunt was just waking up. He was fully dressed. He had followed Paul into bed fully dressed. Paul had expected to wake up with the commander buried to the hilt inside him. He wanted him to. Paul had told him so twice while the commander snuggled up to him.

Paul had slept with the commander at last, but Paul never came out of his sheath, and Commander Blunt never took off his pants. The scaliefox did not know what to think about last night.

Blunt turned around. "Paul, I'm glad you're awake."

"Commander?"

He leaned over and held Paul's face. "I needed that. Thank you. I can't even begin to describe what a relief it was to tell someone."

Paul held Blunt's hand. He stammered. "But... But we didn't do anything."

Blunt smiled. "Yes, we did. You did a lot for me."

"I... I don't understand."

He smiled wider. "I hope the universe never changes you. On second thought, I'd rather sell my soul to whatever deity guaranteed *you* could change the universe."

He lowered his head and leaned away. Paul reached up, but the commander had already turned around. He opened the door and walked out. The door shut and locked behind him.

Paul stared at the curtain covering the door. He felt good about last night. He didn't know why, but he liked it.

INT – PAUL'S SHOP / 0630

The door chime rang. Paul was expecting her, so he pushed the button on the console. Aaza parted the curtain. She wasn't wearing an antistatic ESC uniform. In fact, she was only wearing a waistcover, not unlike a Grovian's, but cloth. The red-furred wolf smiled as she made her way to the console. Paul stood up to meet her.

"Well," she began. "Today's the day I stop watching."

She embraced him. He embraced her. Being touched made him slide out of his sheath, and the shop had not even opened yet.

She had told him a while ago that she liked the scent in here. Her species didn't understand most human forms of entertainment. New and interesting scents were what she craved, and Paul's shop had some of the most intriguing she had ever come across. The longer she watched, the more scents she took in, the more she daydreamed about it. Just the idea. The possibility.

She removed her waistcover and began applying scent masking oil to her hands and feet. Her body made scent elsewhere, but this would cover most of it. There was still a good possibility she would be recognized visually if anyone stationed on FarS3 entered the room, but if that happened, she had already decided to own what she was doing.

Paul took her through his routine to get ready for the day. Aaza was surprised by how much calibration and maintenance the printer in the back needed. Paul rarely let anyone see him using the machine, and Aaza had always wondered how it worked. Watching Paul clean and maintain the machine and load polymer into it and sort the orders and handle billing made her forget, just for a moment, what Paul actually did all day.

At nine-hundred hours, Paul lit the sign out front and waited for clients. Less than an hour later, a Stozi walked in. Paul set the door to chime and climbed off the bed. This was a returning client, so he seemed a little confused seeing Aaza also sitting on the bed.

"I'm having a sale today," Paul answered. "A female body to try your sleeves on if you wish. No extra charge."

The Stozi appeared unmoved. "And who are you?"

"I'm... *Pauline*," Aaza said, waving her tail. "Paul's apprentice."

"Fascinating," said the Stozi.

He didn't need a new sleeve; he was picking up a next-day order. Paul always made himself available if a client wanted to test a sleeve for quality assurance. Sure enough, he did, but not on Pauline.

The Stozi left, depositing his used sleeve in the receptacle by the door.

Aaza didn't feel bad about it. The day had only just begun. Between clients, Paul worked at the printer, leaving her a little bored, so she got up to help print the orders.

Several new clients came in minutes after they had boxed the last order. This Grovian seemed very interested in her, so she rolled over and lifted her tail, making sure je was wearing a sleeve.

EXT – FARS3, SHIPS DOCKING AND UNDOCK-
ING. DOCKING AND UNDOCKING. DOCKING AND
UNDOCKING. DOCKING AND UNDOCKING.
DOCKING AND UNDOCKING AS THE RIFT BE-
HIND THE STATION PULSES FASTER AND
FASTER

INT – PAUL'S SHOP / 1430

The human pulled out of her. Aaza rubbed muzzles with Paul kneeling on the bed next to her, still underneath a client, another human, part of the military armada patrolling the rift. Aaza wondered if this human and the Grovian watching from against the wall were together.

She felt someone else climb up behind her and push in. Aaza hung her head. She had always wondered how it felt to be used, one male after another, no breaks, just freely available to anyone who wanted somewhere to put their cock.

She'd lost count of how many people had used her in the last few hours. Some tried to talk to her, but by now she was mindless. She barely felt anything they were doing now, and she wondered if Paul did. He must, or he wouldn't be here.

She imagined what it must be like for Paul, to want it all the time and never need to connect with anyone; the feeling was all that mattered.

For a few brief hours, she understood Paul.

When this group of humans and Grovians left, she collapsed on the bed. She almost fell asleep, but Paul nudged her.

"You smell like me now."

Aaza laughed and rolled to her back. She was thankful sleeves were required in here, or she would have felt extremely dirty.

"Aren't you tired? Don't you feel satisfied now?"

He licked her muzzle. "Satisfied?"

"Oh, Paul, who are you?"

Paul lay on his stomach and sighed. "I like dreaming."

Aaza stood up. Her legs wobbled and she had to lean on the bed to stay standing. She laughed. "How do you do it?"

"It's what I was made to do."

"What do you mean *made?*"

"It's..." Paul just breathed, closing his eyes.

"I swore I'd make it one whole day, but I'm exhausted. I can't do this anymore." The wolf stood up and stretched, patting Paul on the back. "Thanks so much for letting me try it."

Paul rolled over and curled up.

Aaza had left her waistcover on her table in the corner. She looked it over. She thought of all the days she spent in here, breathing the air.

"Did you like it?" Paul asked.

Aaza turned to him. "I thought I would. I always wondered... Now I think I know. This is why I joined the ESC."

"Hmm?" Paul said, ears flicking.

"Paul, this... This explains everything I've done my whole life. The Hyzr culture—my culture—idolizes control. Nothing happens to anyone without permission. That's probably why my people don't have an empire, let alone a major city. We don't do anything without thinking about how it affects others. My parents couldn't believe I'd want to join the ESC when our planet isn't even a member. My family tried to stop me, but there was something about it. Just the idea of having to take orders from people I'll never meet, from people who don't care how their orders affect me. It sounded so exotic I had to join. I had to experience it. The longer I watched you, the more I realized it was a surrogate for feelings I never wanted to admit I had. Fantasies I lived over and over but was always told they were forbidden. Watching what you do all day... It took me all these years to admit I was jealous."

Paul licked his lips and opened his eyes. "I like letting other people control me. Things make more sense."

Aaza had put on her waistcover. She walked over to Paul and licked him on the muzzle. "I could force myself to go the rest of the day, but I have to admit it. I'm disappointed. This last hour, I was bored. In my mind, it feels so good, but actually doing it... It's not what I imagined. Maybe this is why I haven't been enjoying my enlistment with the ESC either. I live the fantasies in my mind for hours at a time. It's an exciting idea, giving up your body to anyone who wants it, but... It just doesn't feel as good as I imagined, and I can't stay here any longer waiting for it to start."

"Mmmmm. Will you still have coffee?"

Aaza smiled. "Maybe. The scents *are* entertaining."

He licked her on the muzzle. "Do you want my credits for the day?"

She laughed. "Half the day. What the hell. I think I earned them. Thanks again. I wish it felt the way I imagine. I envy you."

She exited. Paul sighed and waited for his next client. He missed having her scent in here already.

INT – PAUL'S SHOP / 0900

Paul switched on the external sign on his way to the bed. He sat down on it, facing the door. Seconds later, the door chimed. Paul's tail wagged. He always enjoyed it when people visited him first thing in the morning, as usually it was a nocturnal species, and they were fascinating to be with.

"Enter."

The computer unlocked the door. The curtain parted, and in walked Commander Blunt, followed by Lieutenant Aaza Kas-sti. Then Z-rank Sela Jar'i. Then Doctor Lawrence Dorset, still very much white and heterosexual, despite now being married to Systems Update Specialist Ihara. The Fißeri followed. He was without a clutch of eggs, the most recent operating system update, version 124.61a, having broken the lighting controls and ventilation system, leaving Ihara to keep them running by hand until version 124.62 came out one week later. Then Cylinder, in a transparent, humanlike form. It had been doing this lately to demonstrate its loyalty to the Universe of Dead Water. Finally, Riack, carrying some strange piece of equipment under one arm. They stood in a semicircle in front of the bed. The door closed and locked.

Commander Blunt spoke. "Computer, seal the door. Disable chime."

Paul blinked. His tail fell and dangled off the bed. Everyone was staring at him. Riack had set up the device on a small table. Paul sniffed it from a distance but still didn't recognize it.

Blunt: "Good morning, Paul. We need a word with you, and this is very important. Kas-sti."

The red wolf wearing the ESC uniform addressed the scaliefox. "I had a hunch about that profile of the Setjalar you made. I've been studying it for weeks."

A few people in the semicircle giggled.

"*Purely* in the interest of scientific research," she continued, though her tail swished a couple times. "The winding pattern around the shaft and knot intrigued me and I wondered how it could be natural. Then at some point I noticed the subtle back and forth movements in the path, and it reminded me of something I saw from Earth. Phonographic audio storage. So I fed the groove path through an audio converter, and something started playing. It was so interesting I had the computer print a vinyl disc and delete all digital traces of my research."

Blunt spoke. "Play it."

Riack pushed a button. A plate on top of the machine began to spin. The hairless feline then lowered the upper arm of the device onto the rotating piece. Sound came from the device, and a woman's voice filled the room.

Setjalar, created from the DNA of fifty-seven species of sentient and nonsentient life, my most complex work to date.

Paul screamed and fell over on the mattress, curling up and burying his muzzle in his stomach. He tried to cover his ears as he screamed again to drown out the sound.

A manifestation of the perfect soldier. Needs no food. No water. No sleep. Only orders, and for the sake thereof, he will obey without regard for his own life. The Setjalar is strength and power combined with absolute submission to authority—two diametric qualities expected in and required of a soldier taken to each extreme, one physical, the other mental, but each the same, in order to reveal them, inviting the viewer to question the nature of power, and who really possesses it. Signed, Allele. List of other works follows, no particular order, just some of my favorites. Special message after, for those clever enough to find my signature.

Paul felt three hands patting and stroking his leg, two stroking his arm, and two feeling his face and neck, all moving from his fur side to his scales and back again.

"Paul, do you recognize this voice?" Blunt said.

The woman's voice continued. *Construct One, half reptile, half mammal, genes from eight species. Construct Two, same. Construct Three, same...*

Paul cried and writhed under their hands as she spoke.

"Pause," Blunt said.

Riack lifted the arm off the disc, and the voice fell silent. Paul calmed down and enjoyed being touched again.

Sela had her feathery hand on his arm, gently squeezing it. "You know this voice, don't you? Who is she?"

Paul shook. He clamped his muzzle shut and closed his eyes.

Ihara was touching his leg. Feeling scales against his scales would normally have been a nice experience. "I'm sure it's painful, but we need you to face this. We'll help you."

Paul clenched his eyes shut.

Doctor Dorset was heterosexually stroking the fur on his leg. "You've told people you were a Construct. This person used the same word. She's describing people like you. Do you know her?"

Paul sobbed. They weren't going away this time. They weren't leaving him.

At once, their touches aroused him. Every touch aroused him. All nerves in his body were connected to his groin in some way. He focused on that and opened his eyes.

"Concentrate on me if it helps," Cylinder said, in a transparent Grovian body now, caressing Paul's muzzle. "I know what it's like to grow up as a lab experiment."

The Construct nodded. His jaw muscles had locked in place, and it took effort to make his mouth move.

"She created me."

Paul was starting to come out of his sheath feeling all these hands on him. Nobody seemed to notice.

"Is she is a scientist?" the doctor asked. "A terrorist?"

Paul shook his head slowly, fighting the tremors. "An artist."

"Artist?" Several of them said it at once.

"It's her hobby," Paul said. "Twenty-nine of us. Same... profile."

"Genetic profile?" Doctor Dorset asked, in that manner only a heterosexual person could.

Paul nodded.

Blunt began, feeling the fur and scales around his neck. "The same person who created you also created the Province's army. We need to know everything we can about her. What happened to you?"

Paul closed his eyes and convulsed again. "Please no."

The hands gently rolled him over, and they began rubbing his underside. Several hands were rubbing his sheath and testicles. He came out of his sheath. Gradually Paul stopped shaking, and he breathed normally.

"Allele," Paul began. The hands slowed but still remained in contact. The touches felt so good. "She made us. Just... playing around with genes. She designed us to couple with one another all the time. We were born grown up. The first thing I can remember is overpowering lust. For my first years of life, it was all I could think about. All we did. She took us on tour. Audiences watched us. She showed everyone what she could do."

"On tour?" Sela said. "Where?"

Paul was convulsing. "I don't know. It was so wonderful. The good feelings."

"Then what?" Aaza prompted.

"She sent us away."

"She mentions a few celestial events," Aaza said. "I've dated the recording to just forty years in the past. Is that right?"

"Yes. She said she had to send us away."

Commander Blunt was still feeling the fur behind his neck. "At the end of the recording she implies she had purchased an exhibition hall on a world in sector three-one-eight. That's halfway across the galaxy. She kept all of these creations on permanent display, including you. But if the Setjalar were an art project, why are they out there fighting us? How did you get here? Why did she send her creations away?"

Paul nodded. "I don't remember. I was created to have sex. I was created to think about nothing else. If not for the Atlins figuring out how I can use this to make money, I don't know where I would be."

"You've been keeping this inside of you for years," Cylinder said, transparent reptile hand feeling behind Paul's ears. It was keeping itself rigid for Paul's sake. "Paul, I'm..."

"She ended it!" Paul howled. "I was happy! I loved the other Constructs, and she took them away from me! She took paradise away!" He convulsed as he caught his breath. "The Atlins gave it back, as much of it as I could get."

"Paul," commander Blunt began, "Do you realize what this means?"

Paul opened his eyes and looked around at everyone feeling his underside. He noticed his penis had changed from purple to red. The commander continued.

"Our best guess is that Allele either created the Setjalar for the Fluidic Province as a commission, or agreed to let them purchase the DNA pattern for their use. She left sexual function in them because it looked more aesthetic for the perfect soldier to have one. We can take advantage of that. It may be their only weakness. Paul, we intercepted multiple Province messages implying numerous Setjalar were caught copulating with one another and neglecting their duties. Some even questioned why they had to take orders."

Doctor Dorset used his unique heterosexual capability of picking up where the commander left off. "They can't modify the DNA to remove the sexual functions because Allele integrated her signature into numerous critical gene sequences."

Z-rank Sela continued. "Grovian and Stozi forces are blocking the rift, so the Province has to breed more Setjalar here. The best they've been able to do is tell their ranks to kill any soldier caught with his codpiece removed."

Commander Blunt leaned close to Paul's muzzle. "I have a plan. It's safe to assume every Setjalar knows about this. All you have to do is show them. Once they get a taste of it, they will begin to question if there could be more to life than dying for the Fluidics." He smiled from ear to ear. "It has the potential to take down their military from the inside. Without the Setjalar, the Life has nothing, but it all depends on you leaving this room."

The scaliefox couldn't breathe. "No! I don't want to leave! I'm happy here! Out there is... Nothing makes sense! I'm miserable!"

"We can't capture any Setjalar alive," Blunt said. "You'll have to go to them."

"I can't!"

Aaza: "We will help you. You've done so much for everyone on this station all these years it's the least we can do."

Paul was rolling side to side, sobbing. Everyone held him still.

Commander Blunt was holding his face. "If this works, an entire species will welcome you with open arms."

Paul slowed to a stop and rested on his back. He looked down at himself. His penis had changed to white. Nobody had touched it. The idea of going out there and being used by an entire species aroused him.

"I can't be anything else," Paul said, voice small and breathless. "They can't either. Allele designed us that way. I'm not alive. I'm art. I have no place outside a display case."

"I don't believe that," Cylinder said, this time using its mouth to speak instead of vibrating its body.

The hands lifted him up and sat him upright on the bed.

"You'll have to work harder at it," Doctor Dorset said. "Your brain probably is hardwired for one thing, just as the Setjalar's are, but the brains of all species can form new connections."

"Let's get started on that," Blunt said. "Computer, unseal the door. Open and hold."

Everyone lifted Paul off the bed and stood him upright on the floor. Paul's erection was now green, and it throbbed as it jutted out in front of him.

"There is more out there," Cylinder said, still using its saurian mouth to speak. "You've wanted to be part of it for a long time. Now you can have a purpose out there. We will help you. Would you like that?"

Paul stared at the open door. He heard footsteps moving out there.

"You can do this," Aaza said.

"You're overdue for a vacation anyway," Riack said.

Paul panted and yet still felt like he was about to pass out. He looked down at himself. It had changed from green to pink. He stepped forward. All seven people around him held his arms and walked with him.

Paul took another step.

He took three steps and stood at the curtain. Aaza held the curtain aside for him. Paul saw the inner diamond. He convulsed, and yet he remained out of his sheath and throbbing. A hint of black was rising through the pink.

"We'll go to the med-lab first," Doctor Dorset said. "I'll do a full medical exam, I'll use my heterosexual medical skills in a completely heterosexual way to examine your biology in great detail. Is that all right? We still know almost nothing about you."

Paul looked at him. To go on a mission. To be part of the adventures he had only heard about. The idea of going out there to make the galaxy into the paradise he had lost so long ago made Paul's erection flush from pink to solid black. The chance to have more of that feeling intrigued him.

Paul took a step.

INT – HADRON'S BAR

The bird wore nothing but leather straps and metal rings today. He had been told it was bondage gear in human culture, but Hadron thought it could be the next archetypal apparel for a bartender. Plus, it highlighted his feathers well, something species with visual aesthetics would see as professional.

He poured the red liquid from the spiral-shaped bottle. The patron at the bar practically owned this seat, but at least he didn't drink the same thing every day, and he always paid in cash.

"Something I've wanted to ask you," Hadron said. "I see you here every day, when most people are just waking up. What exactly do you do for money?"

Zern was about to answer, but Hadron held up his feathered hand.

"Wait, I know it's rude ask that question. It breaks several Laws of Customer Experience, but I think a breach of etiquette is in order. Not that I'm complaining. It's just that for years I've been wondering how a person with a single cargo ship earns enough cash for Atlin, human, and Stozi wine, *and* has the freedom to begin drinking a bottle at nine o'clock in the morning and not finish until thirteen hundred hours."

Zern took a sip of the red liquid.

Hadron leaned in close. "You can tell me. I keep lots of secrets. You wouldn't believe some of the things people have told me. I'd let you in on some of them, but that's why they're secrets."

Hadron smiled with his eyes. He noticed movement beyond the giant insect sipping wine and focused past him. His eyes widened.

"Turn around very, very slowly. Don't make any sudden movements or loud noses. You might startle him."

Zern swiveled on the stool and stopped mid-sip. He rose from the chair, wineglass still tilted up to his mouth.

One by one the other patrons at the bar, mostly nocturnal species about to retire for the day, rose from their seats. A hush drifted over the establishment. A few people cautiously approached the rail. They barely breathed as they stared, drinks in hand.

Even at night, Hadron had never witnessed the bar become this quiet. In the back of his mind, he knew he needed to end the betting pool and check the records for the winner. It had been so long since he started taking bets on when that half reptile half dog would finally come out of his shop he couldn't remember what the jackpot was up to. Twice he began to look away and walk to the terminal to pull up the information, but each time he hesitated and

watched as the senior officers led Paul around the inner diamond.

Hadron smiled. He decided to clear the tabs of every
person at the bar. It felt like the right thing to do.

INT – INNER DIAMOND

So many scents out here. Paul recognized most of
them, and he instantly pictured the profile associated with
each—his mind became flooded with their shapes and their
locations in the database and what people had told him
while this one or that one had been in him.

The hands guided him to turn, and Paul followed their
lead. Each step felt like setting foot on a new planet. People
on the inner diamond stopped walking and backed against
the wall. Everyone at Hadron's bar was watching.

Paul looked and scented around. He recognized so
many faces and scents. He was shaking and barely able to
put one foot in front of the other. He was still out of his
sheath, black, close to climax. The hands held him upright
and walking. Paul stumbled so many times—all the scents
flooded his mind with images of their penises and how
much he desired to have them under his tail.

Every single person on the inner diamond was standing against the bulkheads, silent as the vacuum of space.
Paul heard a few people whispering not to make any sudden movements, not to startle him.

Everyone Paul saw was smiling. Paul wagged his tail in
reply. The body contact helped him focus on walking. The
crew led him around, and now he saw the med-lab. He had
not been here since the station was a holographic customer
service call center run by Atlins. The hands led him inside.

INT – MEDICAL LAB

All these hands touching him and now being in a new place had finally pushed Paul over the edge, and he ejaculated as soon as the door closed. Doctor Dorset grabbed a beaker and held it just under the tip, collecting as much of it as he could as it came out. Paul filled the beaker, but Aaza had another one ready, and she continued collecting as Paul panted and gasped, sniffing as he looked around.

Beakers weren't enough. Someone grabbed a bucket. Paul stood still and filled it to just shy of the brim, relieved he wouldn't have to pay for cleaning beams this time.

Doctor Dorset remained heterosexual and white even after all of this.

EXT – ESTABLISHING SHOT OF FAR SPACE 3, RIFT PULSING MAJESTICALLY BEHIND IT

INT – CONFERENCE ROOM / 1430

Commander Blunt sat in the chair at the head of the table, holding a tablet and tapping through the contents. Doctor Dorset, standing in a way that reminded the commander of his whiteness and heterosexuality, looked at the far wall as he spoke.

"I have run a full medical panel, as requested, including a DNA profile and a neurological scan. The DNA matches the description we heard on the, uh, the recording from Allele. I can detect eight separate species that make up his genome, five sentient, three animal. As for his mental profile, I'm afraid I don't have good news. The brains of species that are products of natural evolution have neural connections branching in all directions. Practically every neuron is connected to its neighbors in some way. Paul's mind is unlike anything I've ever seen before. I would have to call it a work of art. Most of Paul's neural pathways are routed to his pleasure center. He's absolutely right, sir. He was created to live in an artist's display and copulate with other Constructs. He has a one-track mind in every sense of the word."

"Doctor, I hope you're not suggesting what I think you're suggesting."

"In my professional opinion as a heterosexual cis white male doctor with the Democratic Earth & Space Command Committed to Peace and Democracy, Construct Twenty-Three, better known as Paul, is incapable of comprehending much of anything else. His neural pathways are simply too streamlined to form connections beyond it."

"Can you help him?"

"Commander, take a look at the diagram in section four."

Blunt found the image of the inside of a skull and dragged his finger across it. The image rotated, and at first he didn't notice anything unusual, but at one angle he saw something. He turned it back, and sure enough he saw a pattern that resembled tree leaves. He rotated the image around. The leaves gradually morphed into a face, possibly a self-portrait. He did not recognize the species. As he turned the image, the face dissolved into a series of short lines that rotated and interlocked to form letters in an unfamiliar written language. Blunt had a feeling it was a signature.

"Quite a work of art," Doctor Dorset said. "Those are neural pathways you're looking at. Invisible to the naked eye, but they will show up on a neural scanner. I wish I could meet her so I could ask her how she did it."

Blunt tossed the tablet ten centimeters away. It clacked on the table. "That's Paul's brain. Not just a work of art. He has to live with whatever she did to him."

"I only mean to say that it's amazing she was able to create aesthetic patterns out of living tissue *and* a sentient creature with a specific purpose in mind."

"I need to know if Paul is capable of survival outside that room."

"It's as we suspected for years. Paul views everything in sexual terms. His brain is hardwired to do so. When he sees the number five, he might comprehend one more than four, but he's going to see a Jakozian phallus first. If you were to read a history of Telose to him, he would be constantly wondering what each person's reproductive organ looks like and how it might feel inside him. My guess is he doesn't understand someone or something unless it has a reproductive organ he can feel in his mouth or... Well, that's how his mind categorizes and sorts information."

"Doctor."

"The short answer is no, I don't believe he can survive outside that room. Alone. Evolution equips all life forms with the ability to observe their environment and react to stimuli within it. Paul doesn't have that. He has no survival instinct. He was designed to be in a room and copulate. That's his environment, and he has limited capacity to understand anything else."

"But he can learn."

"Certainly. He learned how to use his contraceptive machine. He understands bookkeeping and the concept of money. Forgive the comparison, sir, but you can teach a house cat to use a toilet, but that doesn't imply the cat can learn quantum physics. Paul has the same number of neurons we do, but most of them are arranged in specific patterns and connected along one path. He can learn within his area of expertise, but not far beyond it. For example, he can analyze a male reproductive organ and he can translate that information into three-dimensional coordinates to produce a model just as detailed and fast as our main computer. He's a super genius in a handful of very specific areas. Outside of those areas may well be outside his comprehension."

Blunt took a deep breath through his nose. "At least now we know what we're working with. He clearly wants to leave that room and be part of life on the station. He doesn't know how, but he feels it. We owe it to him to help him go as far as he is able."

"A little fresh air would do him some good, but if he's in combat, he won't know what to do. He has no fight or flight instinct. He views everyone as a potential mating partner. He doesn't understand someone unless he has mated with them. You can teach him new things if you frame them in sexual terms, or if they relate to sex in some way. And sir, we're dealing with the same artist here. It's entirely possible the Setjalar have a similar brain structure. They may also be incapable of comprehending reality in any terms other than war."

"That's not what Paul described. He reached them. He showed them something new, and they neglected obedience for the sake of it. Paul shows all the same signs."

"I'd say he's perfect for this mission. If anyone can get the Setjalar to risk their lives by taking their armor off, it's Paul, but I cannot stress this enough, Commander. He has no capacity to survive outside his room. He will need people around him to keep him safe."

"That's all I needed to know. Thank you, doctor."

Doctor Dorset turned and walked out of the room. Blunt picked up the tablet and skimmed it again.

"Blunt to Sela."

Go ahead, commander.

"Z-rank, our heterosexual doctor has given me his medical opinion on our operative. He's going to need special handling. Namely, he will need people to look out for him. Can I count on you?"

Aye, sir, but I hope you're planning to send more than just me.

"That I am, Z-rank. I'm working on a mission briefing right now. I'll call you when it's ready. Blunt out."

Commander Blunt rubbed his temple and looked out the window at the pulsating rift in the distance. It took him back to his childhood on an ESC research station set up in orbit around a black hole, watching entire stars speed by, whip around the empty space where the universe ended, and then fling back around. He spent hours watching stars and planets move too fast to comprehend.

His parents told him over and over those objects he could see were unreachable—the black hole was deadly—the planets were uninhabitable—the gravity at work was so strong it would tear anyone apart being anywhere close to these places.

Maybe that's why he had fallen in love with the view. It had been so spectacular he remembered being bored by stationary stars when his family transferred to Earth. He smiled thinking if he hadn't craved that view again, he never would have joined the ESC, and he wouldn't have volunteered to move to the newly acquired station near Telose.

The rift pulsed. The universe as he knew it ended there. It seemed just as lethal as a black hole. He was home.

INT – REBEL BRIDGE

Blunt stood beside the commander's chair, addressing everyone. Only nine people onboard this ship, all of them gathered on the bridge. Paul clung to Cylinder, who had taken on the form of a Grovian. The face was featureless, and it had no scent. The only articulate thing on the Fluidic's body was the piece jutting out from its midsection. It had recreated Akaak's profile, and it was the only part of itself it kept completely solid. For the first time anyone had seen, Cylinder had changed its color to mimic the flat scales of a Grovian. The penis was the only part of it that was completely opaque. Cylinder seemed to be trying to make its entire body opaque, as the colors kept swirling around and fading in and out, often in time with Paul's motions. Sucking it or grasping it helped calm Paul down as he observed the new environment. Just seeing it was often enough to calm his nerves.

"We commence our mission to stick a wedge into what is apparently the only crack in the Fluidic Province's war machine: that their soldiers will begin to question why they are soldiers. They obviously can't change the genetic profile of the Setjalar, so they have essentially made abstinence a command, and tasked the Setjalar to enforce it on one another. They have introduced fear of one another into their ranks. That's something we can exploit. Our mission is to sneak our small team into Province territory so our operative can show them the benefits of disobedience. Once word of this spreads, it will destabilize their military.

"We are to avoid combat. Our mission is to link up with an Atlin resistance cell and deliver our operatives. Nothing more. Most of you are here in case something goes wrong. In that scenario, we are to fight quickly and get away. Once we deliver our operatives..."

Blunt spared a glance at Paul. He was sucking Cylinder's Grovian penis. Cylinder was rubbing Paul's head. The commander cleared his throat.

"Once we deliver them, we can go home. Feel free to say prayers for us. I want nothing to go wrong. I want this war to end as much as all of you do. This is our chance to make it happen. Everyone, to your posts."

The formation broke. Paul released Cylinder's fake erection and clung to its waist, facing the commander. Blunt walked up to him and rested a hand on his shoulder.

"Did you hear that?"

Paul nodded. "Yes, I understand. I'll be brave out there. I promise."

Blunt smiled. "I know you will. You'll be in your element, just in a different room. You can do this."

Cylinder led him out. It actually used its legs to simulate locomotion. Blunt smiled as he took a seat in the commander's chair.

"Helm, set course for Atlina Prime."

INT – REBEL CABIN

The Rebel's crew cabins were mere bunks. This ship was designed for combat, not comfort. Nonetheless, Cylinder and Paul sat in a corner. The Fluidic had changed form to mimic the appearance of a Setjalar, without armor, complete with opaque feathers and a lengthy erection emerging from an avian slit. Paul was licking it.

"Does this really help you concentrate?" Cylinder said.

"Things make more sense when penis is involved."

"I'm very sorry you were brought into the world this way. It's one thing to grow up in a lab. Another thing entirely to be engineered to stay in one."

"I like it."

"I've always wondered if you felt trapped in your shop. If you were unable to leave."

"I never really wanted to leave. Oh, sometimes I did. When the station was shut down. Days when I saw no new clients and just stood at the machine filling orders, hoping someone would come through the door. Hearing about things going on elsewhere."

"Why didn't you come out? Why didn't you tell anyone what had happened to you?"

"I just wanted the good feelings to last forever."

"You would have been welcomed."

"I was happy in there. Things made sense. Now I'm traveling. I'm traveling again. I'm on a mission."

"A mission you're uniquely suited for."

Paul's tongue was hyper aware of the fingerprint-like groove wrapping around the shaft and knot. Cylinder had duplicated it exactly.

"It makes me wonder," the Fluidic continued. "The Setjalar are out there fighting the Province's war. You said Allele sent the Constructs away. She never said why?"

Paul mumbled *no* with a full muzzle.

"The Setjalar are doing what they were designed to do. Perhaps the Constructs are as well. Maybe she was not being calloused when she sent you away."

Paul looked up at it, still with a full muzzle.

"I like to think she knew she couldn't keep you there forever, so she found homes for all the Constructs, just as she found a home for the Setjalar. She likely sent you here on purpose."

Paul stopped sucking but did not release the organ. It felt so real, and now it looked real. That Cylinder had become opaque for Paul made him feel special.

"Take comfort in that," Cylinder continued. "Perhaps she thought you would be useful on Far Space 3."

Now he released Cylinder. "Even if she didn't, I'm happy where I am."

Cylinder rubbed Paul between his ears. "Don't resent your mother, but don't hide from your feelings toward her either. They will haunt you for the rest of your life, whether you're aware of them or not."

Paul leaned into its hand.

EXT – THE REBEL, CRUISING AT HYPER

INT – REBEL BRIDGE

Z-rank Sela was staring at the tablet in her fingers. Aaza was next to her.

"This is impossible," Sela said.

"It seems reasonable to me," answered the wolf.

"Once we meet up with the Atlin Strikers, we're supposed to travel to find Life activity at major oceans in Atlin territory and then introduce their Setjalar forces to Paul. How? They never allow themselves to be captured alive, and we can never get close enough to them to sneak anybody inside. Paul will be shot if he's discovered inside one of their camps."

"Sela, you were customer service. If there's one thing you know how to do, it's give people passive-aggressive hell."

"Somehow I have to make it happen. Aaza, I have no idea how I'm going to do this. The weight of the war is on my shoulders. I think everyone expects this to be how the war ends, and I haven't even worked out how I'm going to get our operative in."

"You also helped destroy ten Customer Support Stations. I hear Far Space 3 only survived because the bomb malfunctioned. Now it's become a center of diplomacy."

"What's your point?"

"You saw how the Setjalar behaved around Paul. It won't take much effort to convince them to come close. If a detail here or there doesn't work, the plan will end up better for it."

"One wrong move and he's dead. Then what? Travel the galaxy and patrol every single ocean on every single planet? How do you keep liquid people away from water? And why would we need to?"

"What do you mean?"

"Those are my orders. Seek out places where the Life is trying to raise the oceans and disrupt them. Get Paul into contact with the Setjalar in the area. If this is some ridiculous idea, why is the Dead Water Alliance making disrupting their efforts a priority?"

"You think there might be something to it? The Life's plan to resurrect the oceans?"

"Cylinder is here... What if it didn't come from the other side?"

Aaza thought for a moment. "We've been assuming this is crazy. But... Maybe there's a reason they've created an entire army to help them."

"That's what I'm thinking. What if there's something Command isn't telling us?"

"Maybe you can find out while you're taking Paul around. You're the ideal person for this mission. Never forget that."

"Glad someone has confidence in me because—"

The ship listed to the left.

Blunt braced himself in his chair, wondering why ESC ships did not have seat belts. "Report!"

Aaza struggled to see the screen as the ship rocked back and forth. "Two Setjalar ships are firing on us."

"How the hell did they detect us?"

Another shot. The ship rocked again. A wall panel overloaded and sparked.

"Sir, we're dropping out of hyper."

Blunt: "Damn it! Evasive pattern theta! Engine room, get the hyperdrive back online!"

EXT – THE REBEL DROPPING OUT OF HYPER, FLANKED BY TWO SETJALAR SHIPS

INT – REBEL BRIDGE

The ship rocked again. Another panel sparked, and the crewmember at the station flew backwards and landed on her back.

"Targeting systems are offline," Aaza shouted.

"Aim manually!" Blunt yelled. "Return fire!"

EXT – THE REBEL RETURNS FIRE, DAMAGING ONE OF THE PROVINCE SHIPS. BOTH SHIPS FIRE BACK, BLASTER FIRE BURNING A LINE DOWN THE TOP OF THE REBEL

INT – REBEL BRIDGE

The ship rocked back and forth. Sparks flew everywhere. Crew members lay on the floor in agony.

Somehow Blunt had managed to stay seated. "Engine room!"

No response.

Aaza had also managed to remain seated at her station. "Shields are gone. Engines are gone. Weapons are at half power."

Less than a second later, four Setjalar teleported onto the bridge. Blunt stood up and unholstered his handlaser, but a Setjalar soldier fired into his shoulder before he could. Blunt went down and lay motionless on the floor.

The soldiers shot every single person on the bridge and then turned to enter the corridor.

INT – REBEL CORRIDOR

Three teams of four Setjalar each moved through the ship, going from room to room, shooting everyone on sight.

One team came to a bunk. Cylinder was still in a Setjalar form, and Paul was still suckling him.

The three soldiers all aimed their rifles at them. They hesitated. Cylinder was giving a marvelous performance as he imitated the moans and motions of a flesh-and-blood life form being stimulated.

The feathery canine stepped forward, not sure what to make of this scene.

Cylinder tapped Paul on the head, indicating he was about to imitate ejaculation. Paul understood what it meant. He opened his mouth just as liquid was about to come out. Cylinder gasped and panted, giving an excellent performance.

The soldiers trained weapons on him. Paul lay on top of the Fluidic and licked its muzzle. The soldiers looked on through their rifle scopes.

Paul looked at them and felt Cylinder's chest and abs. It had no armor on, which would have alerted the soldiers. It was a risk, Cylinder knew it, and so did Paul, but they also hoped the Setjalar would be more curious than repulsed seeing one of their own basking in afterglow.

Paul faced them. He licked his lips. All three of them smelled enticing, and he wanted to have them under his tail. He felt Cylinder up and down, hoping the approaching soldiers would consider the possibility that this could be them. Cylinder was doing a remarkable job imitating climax, not to mention maintaining opaqueness.

The soldiers lowered their weapons. The door closed behind them. All three of them looked around. They seemed to check with one another, and they removed their codpieces at the same time. Paul licked his lips and walked on his hands and knees up to the group. He nuzzled the inside of the middle soldier's thigh. With his other two hands, he felt up the inside of the other soldier's legs.

Their dicks slipped out at the same time. Paul gripped the two on either side of him while suckling the one by his muzzle. After a few seconds on this one, he licked the one on his left from base to tip, and then the one on his right. Judging by how their disciplined stances faltered, he must have convinced them he was no threat.

They stood in place and shuddered. The one on the right looked back. He then raised his rifle and fired a blast directly at Cylinder's chest. The Fluidic created a burn mark over its chest, then slumped over and played dead.

In one motion they secured their codpieces, though they did not fit properly with their cocks jutting out, and the one on the right pushed a button at his ear. Paul felt a conversion beam falling over him. He hadn't been inside one in so long he almost forgot to hold still.

Cylinder couldn't hold this shape anymore. It reached for a communicator.

"Cylinder to Blunt."

Go ahead.

"Mission accomplished."

Acknowledged. Do you require medical assistance?

"I'll be all right, commander."

Well done.

Cylinder lay still. It let its color go as it gasped and began to melt. Cylinder wondered why the Setjalar had not beamed it aboard as a rescue. Perhaps they wanted no witnesses outside their own unit. It hoped Paul would be all right alone. It smiled thinking that their resident Construct was exactly where he needed to be.

And probably exactly where he wanted to be as well.

9

INT – SETJALAR CARGO HOLD / 1100

Setjalar vessels were utilitarian. There was no recreation area. No crew quarters for sleeping. No food. The entire ship was comprised of a bridge, an engine room, and cargo space.

Paul remembered Doctor Dorset talking about the Setjalar, how they were bred for combat, and the pink vial clipped to their chest plates was their sole source of nutrients—formulated to be exactly what their bodies needed so there would be no waste, and thus no need for lavatories. They were free to devote every waking thought for war, as the vials also contained chemicals that replenished neurons, eliminating the need for sleep.

The Setjalar who had carried Paul to this cargo hold only said that he was a Fourth rank, and he had to hide him here. Paul lay on the floor, out of sight, hoping the Setjalar did not have a keen sense of smell. Hours later, one of the other three he had met on the Rebel came back in. Voice low, and moving quietly, he opened a container and gestured Paul over. Paul peered over this soldier's shoulder and observed packaged rations in the crate.

"We took these from your ship," he had said. "Use them wisely. We may not be able to resupply for some time."

Paul nodded. "And..."

He turned to Paul, rising to full height and towering over the scaliefox. "For your other biological needs, you'll have to use one of these empty containers. We'll teleport it off the ship periodically."

"Thank you. What is your name?"

"Fifth rank. It's best if you don't know our names in case we are caught. Our First and Second are not onboard at the moment. We are waiting for the right moment to introduce you to them. Currently I, Sixth, and Fourth are the only ones who know you're here."

He smiled as he reached down and felt Paul's cheek. Paul closed his eyes and leaned into it. The sensation of being touched made him slip out of his sheath.

"The Life is keeping something from us," Fifth said. "It will be easier if you approach other Setjalar and show them. If I tried to do it, they'd shoot me as soon as I touched them. The three of us are of the opinion that others need to know about this."

Paul reached between his legs and felt the codpiece. Fifth spread his legs. Paul unclasped the strip of armor and felt his slit. The lips separated and a ridged shaft slid out. Paul suckled it and moved back as it emerged the rest of the way. He knew exactly where the sensitive spots were, and the knot swelled just seconds after Paul had wrapped his tongue around it.

Fifth's hands rested on either side of Paul's mouth. Paul closed his eyes and let the labyrinth of ridges on the shaft become his universe. Fifth had finished in just a couple minutes. Since every Setjalar penis was the same, Paul was in fact in control of how long each Setjalar lasted. He could make one cum in ten seconds, or he could make them last two hours if he so desired. This time he brought this soldier to climax quickly, as they were not among friends.

He pulled back, and Paul stared at Fifth as it slid back into his slit. Fifth knelt down to be at Paul's eye level, feeling his cheeks. Paul scented his muzzle and felt the feathers on his arms.

Fifth was still panting. "This does not serve the Life, and yet it fills me with all sorts of desires. The Life does not want us to experience them. There are many among our ranks who want to know why. Help us find them."

His touch alone made Paul's throbbing cock change color from purple to red to white. "I want to be held. I want someone inside me all the time. I never want it to end."

"We'll try to accommodate you. I think you may be the best person to teach others about this."

He had risen to full height. Paul remained on the floor, looking up at him. The soldier had retracted into his slit, and he clasped the codpiece back in place.

"Remain quiet and hidden. One of us will call you if we're bringing you a guest. Otherwise, you must do exactly as you are told if you want to survive."

It had been three days since he had seen another person. The ship had been in hyper this whole time, and Paul wondered where they were going. This had been an endurance test for Paul, going multiple days without someone touching him. He expected this to be difficult, but nothing could have prepared him to be without for so long.

Paul ate very little and passed the time picturing his favorite profiles in his mind. Grovian, Enegi, Jakoz, Telosen, human... He missed the variety, and sometimes all he could think about was that all he had to look forward to was the same thing over and over. He had been told this would be work, and now he understood what the word meant. His shop had been a pleasure to run. This would be a mission deep inside enemy territory. Paul's tail wagged thinking he was a member of the ESC now, a soldier, a spy—part of Far Space 3's crew.

Paul was thinking about Akaak's profile when the door slid open. He opened one eye and listened closely. He had taken position at the back, behind several large polymer crates, so he wouldn't be seen if someone who wasn't supposed to know about him wandered inside. Paul heard two sets of footsteps. His mind had associated the sound of Setjalar steps with their profile, and he pictured those fingerprint ridges in his mind, traced them subconsciously.

The footsteps came closer. Paul heard a whisper.

"It's Fourth."

Paul rose from his hiding place and peeked over one of the boxes. He recognized Fourth. Beside him stood another Setjalar he had not seen before.

"Second, this is the one," said Fourth.

"He knows how the Life has been deceiving us?"

"Correct. Let him show you."

Second's eyes narrowed and he turned to Fourth. "You yourself have felt it?"

"I have."

"I am obligated to kill you for even admitting it."

"I was curious why the Life decided to spread fear among us. Let him show you. I'm confident you will understand."

"Obedience brings victory, and victory is our purpose. If I indulge your request, I will be disobeying the Life, which is not my purpose."

"What if there could be more to existence than obedience?"

"That is not possible, Fourth rank. The Life created us to help them achieve victory."

"I have observed you, Second. I have seen you feeling under your armor plating. You wonder why the Life forbade us from removing our armor, too. You're afraid to ask because now we must fear one another. Paul can show you what the Life does not want us to know about ourselves."

Second turned to Paul, who had come out of his hiding spot and was now standing before them. He shook his hips, bouncing his junk for them.

Fourth glanced at Paul and then turned around. "You're afraid this is a trick so I can kill you and get your rank. I'll leave you alone."

He left the room. Paul now stood alone with this strange, feathered canine.

"Paul?" Second said.

Paul nodded, also bobbing from the waist like a bird.

"My Fourth claims the Life is deceiving us."

Paul gulped. "They want you to believe you were created for one purpose, and that's all you can be. The Life didn't create you."

He looked over his shoulder at the door. Then he turned back to Paul. "It is not my place to question why the Life gave such an order. Obedience brings victory, and victory is our purpose."

Paul's tail wagged. He took a step toward Second. "Do you want to know?"

"I do wonder, but that is not the point."

"I know how to remove your armor. You won't be disobeying."

Second did not speak for a moment. Paul was right behind him, taking in his scent. He was glad they did not all smell the same, or this mission would have been boring.

"I suppose you are correct," Second said.

"Then stand still. I will show you."

Second stood at attention as the Construct reached between his legs and unclasped the codpiece. It fell away and dangled freely. Paul felt the slit. Second's disciplined stance melted.

He took Second's entire length down his muzzle. He traced the labyrinth of folds with his tongue. Second stood and panted.

It wasn't very often a client let Paul have control, and Paul decided to use it now. He nudged Second onto his back. The feathery canine obliged and sat on the metal floor. Now Paul could work him easily, and he moved his muzzle back and forth gently, tracing different paths in the labyrinth every stroke.

Second was now lying flat on his back, no longer a soldier, but a person who had just discovered what his body could do, and nothing had prepared him for it.

Paul swung a leg over and straddled his stomach, facing his cock. He worked it from tip to shaft. Eventually the knot swelled, and Paul squeezed it. Paul felt hands reaching up and feeling his fur. He kept working the shaft and teasing the knot. Eventually Second's hips began to buck. Paul moved faster, in time with the hips.

Growling. Snarling. Then heat on Paul's tongue. Setjalar seed was indeed hot and had spice to it. Paul swallowed all of it and sat up, looking back at his client. Still fully armored, Second pulled Paul down. The Construct lowered himself and turned around to lie face to face with him, using one of his pectorals as a rest for his muzzle.

He held Paul close to his chest. "I never imagined disobedience would be desirable."

Paul nuzzled his chest as he felt the muscles up and down his arms, thick enough to pucker his chest even while relaxed.

"What is this?" Second said. "Why do I want to hold you?"

Paul looked up at him. "Because you are more than just a warrior."

Moments later, the door opened. Paul and Second turned to see Fifth, Sixth, and Fourth standing at the entrance.

"They know, too," Paul said.

"If the Life is keeping this from us," Fourth said, "what else are they withholding?"

Sixth spoke up, feathers ruffled. "What if we don't have to die for the Fluidic Province?"

Fifth now spoke. "What if the Life is not worth dying for? Why are we expected to die for them, but they are not?"

"I don't know," Second said.

Fourth smiled. "Come and see Paul whenever you like. Help us bring others. You should now know we have removed one another's armor."

"You have?"

"Fifth is becoming good at this."

"What do you think, Second?" Sixth said.

He held Paul tighter. "I believe I enjoyed this act of disobedience."

The other three stepped inside, removing their codpieces. Fourth already had his hand on Sixth's rear and was rubbing his slit from behind. Paul's tail wagged and he licked his lips.

INT – SETJALAR CARGO HOLD / 1520

The ship was in hyper more often than not. During the times it was not, Paul often received new Setjalar who did not give their name or even rank, and he never saw them again, so Paul figured they must have come from other vessels. He overheard his usual guardians whispering for them to show others. Paul wondered how many soldiers were out there experimenting with disobedience on one another.

Servicing the same profile again and again was starting to bore Paul, but he endured it. He derived pleasure from their different scents. When he asked about cleaning up, he was told there were no such facilities for the Setjalar. Paul felt filthy and unprofessional, but then he remembered he was in a war zone.

He guessed it had been four days since he had shown this ship's Second the new physical sensations and new emotions. Since then, Second had brought Paul many, many Setjalar soldiers. He seemed better at convincing other Setjalar to let Paul remove their codpieces. Thankfully, Paul didn't have to do all the work anymore; once a Setjalar knew how it was done, they were free to play around with one another, and they frequently did so in the cargo hold.

Paul's rations were running low, and he wondered if he would ever have a chance to meet the First, or even a Life—meeting another Fluidic intrigued Paul, and he wondered if Cylinder had, and what meeting others of its own kind had been like.

The ship dropped out of hyper, which woke Paul up out of his light slumber. He sat upright and watched the door from behind the crates. Moments later, the door slid open a crack.

"Find an empty crate and get inside."

The door slid shut again.

That was the voice of Second. Paul had taken note of several empty crates, and he crawled over to one of them now and rolled inside. He had to lie doubled over with his muzzle against his stomach, but he wasn't uncomfortable. He shut the lid over himself and lay in the dark for a moment.

INT – DARK – THE CRATE

Minutes later, he felt a conversion beam, and then daylight and fresh air and outdoor scents seeped through the crack. Paul felt footsteps around him. Setjalar picking up cargo containers and moving them. Someone stood over his box, and Paul heard the lid latch. He held his breath as the box rose into the air and was carried away and placed on top of another cargo box. Paul tested his breath. Only one latch had been closed, so air and light still made their way inside. Paul uncurled as much as he could and lay still.

Footsteps everywhere, at least fifty individuals.

He heard the First rank's voice. "Second ranks, take perimeter. Third ranks take that cover. Fourth ranks..."

Pounding footsteps drowned out his words, and then energy weapon shots began burning the air.

Shouting.

Feathers burning.

Human skin boiling.

People falling to the ground, bones snapping.

Smell of blood.

Paul held his breath as the screams continued and the shouting came closer. An energy blast hit the ground so close he smelled the dirt burning.

He heard footsteps storming closer, and laser blasts gave way to the sounds of fists against flesh.

Something hit his crate, and Paul toppled to the ground. He landed flat and slid a few paces as more cargo hit the dirt around him.

Bodies were falling to the ground as well.

Paul felt fewer footsteps scrambling around.

Sounds of laser rifles being smashed against skulls. Sounds of laser fire burning feathers and skin.

He wasn't sure what all these sounds meant, so he waited patiently for them to stop.

An hour or so later, they finally did. Laser fire halted. The smell of blood and burned skin filled the air in the crate. He heard someone crying in the distance, and then a blast from a laser rifle silenced them.

Footsteps came closer and then stood over Paul's crate. The latch unbuckled, and the lid flipped open. Light flooded Paul's eyes. He was looking up at Third, who held his hand down to Paul. The Construct took his hand and rose to his feet. The view stunned Paul.

EXT – DAY – BATTLEFIELD

Sharp rocks jutted up everywhere from the sandy ground. Many of them had scorch marks where laser fire had hit them. He smelled salt and water in the air but could not see where the scents were coming from.

Bodies lay strewn about, human and Atlin and Setjalar twisted together, blood mixing in the sand. None of these sights and sounds made much sense to Paul, but he did see about thirty Setjalar walking about. Many noticed him and were staring. Paul stood closer to Third.

"First rank is dead," said Third. "So is second. I'm highest rank left."

"What happened?"

"We were directed to retake this planet. ESC forces had overtaken one of our breeding facilities here. We just wiped them out."

Several Setjalar had raised weapons. Other Setjalar were grabbing the guns and lowering them, telling the soldiers to wait. Third was walking Paul into their midst. Paul was scenting the air, trying to filter out the smell of blood and burned feathers to identify the new people.

"We met up with five other units," Third continued. "One hundred and eight altogether. Forty-six survived, but we have retaken the breeding facility."

Third had led Paul into the middle of the camp. Setjalar were approaching him, others holding down their guns and saying things like, "The Life is hiding something from us." "He's helping us. Don't shoot him." "He's a Construct. His name is Paul, and he's here to show you something the Life doesn't want you to know."

"We don't have to hide you now," Third said. "I am in command, and if the Life gives me a rank of First, you will never need to hide again."

Third stopped walking, and now Paul stood against his side, grasping his arm as Third held him around the stomach. The Setjalar in the camp, many bleeding and limping, had gathered around them. Third spoke, gradually turning Paul around for all to see him.

"I am Third rank Tetmar, highest surviving rank in this unit, and I assert my right to command. Paul is an ally, and he is here to show all of you why the Life ordered us to be afraid of one another."

Paul smelled sixteen people he had serviced over the last few weeks among the crowd. They were removing their codpieces right now. A few of the newcomers were backing away, rifles still in hand but pointed down.

"Are you not curious why the Life ordered us to turn our weapons on one of our own if we catch him without his armor on? Since we began fighting for the Fluidic Province, no Life has ever given such an order. We wondered why. Those of you who want to learn why, remove your armor plate. As acting First, I declare no one shall be harmed."

Paul's mouth watered seeing sixteen Setjalar approaching him. He licked his scaly lips. Tetmar, Third rank, had already removed his codpiece. Paul reached up and began rubbing his slit. He emerged from it and stood before all those in attendance.

"We are capable of more than just following orders and dying for the Life," Tetmar said, turning in place to show everyone.

The newcomers were looking at one another, clearly torn between curiosity and loyalty. Paul rubbed everyone's slits in turn, and a minute later he was surrounded by Setjalar penis. The newcomers were looking on. Several of them were reaching for their codpieces.

Four Setjalar standing by raised their rifles at them.

Six soldiers surrounding Paul reached for their pistols at once and fired on the four. Purple laser beams struck them on the head and chest, blasting holes clean through them. Their headless bodies dropped to the ground.

The newcomers turned to the Setjalar around Paul. The Construct had two organs in his hand and one in his mouth, tracing his labyrinth with his tongue.

Sixth addressed them. "No one will be harmed for wanting to know, but there will be consequences for denying others the chance to learn."

The rest of the newcomers set their rifles down and began unbuckling their codpieces. Everyone around Paul made room for them. They didn't need to be rubbed and sucked off. They already knew they'd get a turn on the Construct. Paul raised his tail, eager to be filled by an entire unit of Setjalar soldiers.

10

INT – SETJALAR BREEDING CENTER / 1104

All in a day's work.

Paul had just finished licking this Setjalar to climax. He had only been alive for an hour, having just emerged from an incubation tank, fully-grown and ready to fight. Tetmar and all the other canines Paul had been with over these last few months had agreed this generation of soldiers needed to understand their bodies from the beginning.

Setjalar were born knowing how to handle a rifle. Tactical strategies were encoded in their minds as well. They were capable of understanding complex thoughts from their first breath.

Paul looked down the line of new Setjalar, sixteen of them, all still out of their slits and dripping on the floor. Other soldiers were walking up and down the line, explaining the gravity of what had just happened, and while they were expected to obey all orders given, they were capable of other things as well.

Sometimes walking around such a large building felt scary, but knowing he was surrounded by people who understood him and would use him whenever he needed it helped him get through the days. He was never without someone touching him, and everyone here walked without their codpieces, so Paul frequently walked around with his hand between someone's legs.

They had created over three hundred new soldiers since they arrived. The Life had assigned their unit to secure and run the facility until further notice. Paul had watched the process from beginning to end as a Setjalar went from DNA pattern in a computer to embryo to fully-formed soldier in a matter of hours. Bred for war, they emerged from their tanks asking for orders. Paul wondered if he had been like that when he was created: fully-formed and conscious but instead of orders his first thought would have been to find a partner to mount.

No questions. Just going with whatever his mind had been wired to do.

He watched the Setjalar doing what they were wired to do. Even with the knowledge that they could be something else, they still sought out orders, a place in the ranks, a mission.

He smelled a familiar scent move next to him and place a hand on his shoulder. Tetmar felt his scales and fur. Paul reached up and held his hand as he looked over the new soldiers while they received their ranks and assignments. All of them were to move out to other sectors and join the battles against the Dead Water Alliance. The soldiers gave them extra, secret orders to show other Setjalar what their bodies could do, and until they left, they should explore this amongst each other. No punishment here.

"Tetmar," Paul began. "What would this place be like if we weren't doing this?"

He stood behind Paul, crotch against Paul's fur, arms wrapped around him. "They would be fitted with armor, assigned vials, and then told to join patrols until they were transported to their permanent units. It would look disciplined. None of this casual walking about."

"It sounds scary."

"The soldiers don't need training, but discipline and obedience are reinforced immediately after emerging from the tanks. You certainly wouldn't be walking around freely. Nobody would touch you or speak to you unless they were told to do so by a superior. This casual atmosphere is strange even to me, but I enjoy it. I hope these soldiers will come to appreciate it when they join the ranks."

Paul looked up at him. "Nobody would be with me? They would just stand there?"

He pulled Paul close to his side. "I can imagine what it's like for you. Try to imagine how we comprehend reality."

"I have, but I still don't understand."

"I hope you will someday. I can glimpse how you know reality. I feel it, too. I've observed many others behaving the same way to you, and even among one another. It's something I never imagined experiencing, or wanting to experience. If what you say is true, and the Life did not construct us from nothing, then this may be parts of our genetic ancestry asserting themselves. You must have similar traces within you, as well. Perhaps you will glimpse the reality I was created for."

"I'm not sure if I want to. It scares me."

"This scared me at first, as well. Mostly because I had been ordered not to feel it. I disobeyed, and I am glad I did. The thought of returning to a mindless machine whose only concern is doing what he has been told disgusts me."

He held Paul for another minute. The Construct watched the new soldiers receive their armor and vials and then file out. One of them reached out and felt the slit of the soldier in front of him. He turned and smiled at him, spreading his legs so he could feel better. The pair walked past Paul and Tetmar. Paul's tail wagged.

Moments later, the tanks cleaned themselves, and new DNA patterns were generated and injected into them. Paul stepped forward, Tetmar walking behind him. They passed the tanks, and Paul watched the clumps of cells grow into embryos.

INT – RED LIGHTING – SETJALAR BREEDING CENTER / 1900

An alarm began sounding. The soldier buried to the hilt inside Paul suddenly pulled out. He retracted into his slit almost instantly and secured his codpiece. Paul looked after him as he ran.

As if hearing some command, every Setjalar in the facility migrated to one side of the building. Paul straightened up and stood against the wall, watching. They were all taking rifles and then moving toward the area where the fighter ships were kept. Others were marching to position by the entrances and at regular intervals around the interior.

One of the soldiers stood near Paul, laser rifle held at ready. For the first time, he was standing like a soldier. The Construct walked and stood beside him, against the wall and out of the way.

"What's happening?"

"Dead Water Alliance forces are in orbit. Eight vessels, unknown crew compliment. Our orders are to make sure they do not take this facility."

"But... Aren't we all on the same side?"

"We have our orders."

Paul blinked. He felt sick to his stomach. "All we have to do is tell them what we're doing. Let me speak to them. If they see me, they'll know to help us."

"My orders are to protect this facility."

Paul's heart sped up. He didn't like it when he felt this way. Now would have been a great time for someone to mount him, but he sensed no one would while that alarm sounded.

"Where is Tetmar?"

"During combat, lesser ranks are never told where the higher ranks are."

Paul backed away and ran around the outer wall, scenting the air ferociously. The Setjalar were standing like statues. After living with them for so long, walking among them freely as they lounged around and stimulated one another, Paul had forgotten they were Setjalar.

Paul heard ships taking off and scrambling. Paul weaved between vats of liquid and computer terminals. He smelled only soldiers who had been bred at this facility. He realized everyone else must have boarded the ships and were moving to intercept.

Paul slid to a stop near the middle of the facility, ears folded down as he tried to shut out the alarm. The dim lights reminded him of his shop on Far Space 3, and he desperately wanted to go back there and hide under the covers. He turned in place, tail between his legs as they stood still, all individuality lost, now merely soldiers within a unit within a war.

Finally he opened his mouth and screamed. "Everybody wait! You don't have to do this! I was sent by the Dead Water Alliance! Call them! Tell them I'm here!"

Nobody budged.

Paul turned in place, looking at everyone but no longer able to recognize anyone.

"Please! I'm... I'm giving you an order! Call the ships and tell them we're not their enemy!"

They stood still. Paul couldn't catch his breath.

"You were supposed to learn how to disobey!" Paul shouted. "That's why I'm here! Disobey the Life!"

Paul noticed a few soldiers coming out of attention, and then straightening up again. Paul felt less sick thinking he had reached them after all, but as soon as they showed a sign of independent thought, Paul heard conversion beams all around the building—human, Jakozen, Grovian, and even Atlins appearing, guns ready.

The Setjalar opened fire. The Dead Water Alliance fighters took cover and returned fire. Paul stood in place, looking around, bewildered. He felt a hand on his head shove him to the ground. Paul remained there as laser fire filled the air. He smelled more burning flesh and feathers. Sparks flew. People screamed.

Paul curled up and closed his eyes. Everything outside his shop was so confusing—nobody behaved the way he understood.

In moments, the fighting was over. He heard footsteps coming closer, and Paul opened his eyes to see one of the Setjalar soldiers approaching him. He was bleeding from several laser shots to his shoulder and abdomen, and his armor was so scarred it had broken in multiple places. He stood over Paul and held his hand out. Paul took it and rose to his feet.

Half the Setjalar were dead. All of the Dead Water Alliance forces lay motionless on the floor.

The remaining feathered canines took position around the facility again. All remained quiet. Paul crouched and waited.

Almost an hour later, the alarm went silent, and the lights returned to normal. The soldiers relaxed and began picking up the bodies. The side door opened, and six soldiers emerged from it. Paul recognized their scents as having gone to the ships.

He weaved between pipes and cables and vats and walked with them. They were carrying three wounded between them.

"Is anyone else coming?"

One of the newly bred canines answered. "We are the only ship to survive the attack."

Paul's heart sank. Tetmar was dead. All of the soldiers he had known for months were gone. Paul felt alone. He was in a breeding facility with a bunch of soldiers who were barely two months old. Some had been born mere days ago.

Why?

Paul stopped, let them pass. He stared at the concrete wall as the soldiers lay their wounded down and began treating them.

Paul whispered to himself. "All they had to do was call the ships. They didn't have to die... But they did have to die... They knew we were on the same side, but they still had... to... follow orders. The urge. The desire."

The Construct imagined it. The way he felt about feeling someone under his tail or in his mouth, the Setjalar must feel the same way about obeying orders. They had been created to do that and only that, and it was how they understood reality. He thought about what the Atlins had said about Paul while on Far Space 3, how he was incapable of understanding anything besides a penis—unable to do anything besides desire it. He was trying to teach the Setjalar how to think the way he did, but it would not work that way. He had to show it in a way they would understand. Unless he wanted to lose more soldiers to pointless death, he had to—

"I have to become a soldier," he whispered.

Two Setjalar were standing on either side of him. One touched his shoulder.

"Paul, are you all right?"

The Construct repeated himself, louder. "I have to become a soldier." Paul straightened up and looked at each canine. He spoke loud enough for everyone to hear. "Your First is dead. Your Second and Third are also dead. I assert my rank in this unit."

The two soldiers looked at him. They began to speak. Paul shouted before they could.

"I have been alive longer than any of you! Your First didn't understand what he felt, but I do! We have spread this knowledge to others, and now it's time to use it! We must take over other breeding facilities and prepare soldiers for the time when we will turn against the Province."

"Turn against?" someone said.

"The Life is breeding you to die!" Paul screamed. "You don't have to! That's what this means! You can have desires of your own, and you can live! I am your First! Follow my orders, and you will be free! Follow the Life, and they will send you to your death!"

"We have our ord—"

Paul whirled around and faced the speaker. "They fulfilled their orders, and now they're dead! I showed you what it means to live when you stepped out of the vat! I created you, that makes me your First, and I am showing you what your purpose is!"

Paul had never felt this way before. For the first time in his life, he felt part of a wider reality instead of merely existing in a room.

The Setjalar were looking at one another. One by one they stood at attention facing Paul. The Construct turned in place and observed over fifty Setjalar standing like statues facing him.

As one, they chanted. "Obedience brings victory, and victory is—"

"Stop!" Paul shouted.

The feathered canines stood with their mouths open.

"That's what the Life wants you to say because they want you to accept that you were created to die for them! You can be more than what you were designed to be! Everyone remove your codpieces."

They obeyed, almost in unison. They now stood with that armor plate dangling against one leg. Paul turned in place and made sure everyone was doing it.

"Show me you are alive!"

They rubbed themselves. Paul now had over fifty ridged organs pointing at him.

"You stand before me unashamed of what you are. You are disobeying them, and disobeying the Life will give you life. The Fluidics consider you disposable. I consider each of you fellow Constructs."

Paul scented the room. He found the one he remembered and pointed at him.

"You are the oldest Setjalar here. You are my Second."

He stood up straight. "Yes, First. I swear my allegiance to..."

Paul waited. The soldier had just caught himself about to repeat what he had been designed to say.

The new Second stood tall and began again. "Yes, First. I stand before you unashamed of what I am. I do not desire to die for someone else. I desire my own life, and I swear my allegiance to... to you."

As one, the others repeated. "I stand before you unashamed of what I am. I do not desire to die for someone else. I desire my own life, and I swear my allegiance to you."

Paul stood as tall as he could. He looked down at himself. He was out of his sheath as well, green. He didn't know when he had slid out of his sheath, but for a moment, he thought he understood how the Setjalar felt. He imagined how it felt to be programmed to obey, and to derive the same sense of fulfillment from that as Paul did from being mounted.

Paul understood how it felt to be a Setjalar. Now that he knew how to satisfy them, he felt at home among them.

EXT – PLANET WITH RED CLOUDS AND WHITE OCEANS

Five Setjalar vessels emerged from the planet's atmosphere. Three of them veered left. Two veered right. All of them entered hyper at the same time, speeding away from the planet faster than light.

INT – SETJALAR VESSEL, BRIDGE

Paul was on one of them, standing on the bridge, scared out of his mind. He was mimicking how the Setjalar behaved, and if he let himself think about it, he wanted to curl up in a small room and hide, letting anyone who came inside use him.

So long as he channeled that impulse into acting like a Setjalar, he belonged. He was living their life, fulfilling this desire the way a Setjalar did, and in a strange way, it felt almost the same as being mounted.

They had rebuilt their forces at the facility and left behind instructions for the newly born soldiers. They had a new loyalty now, and they were to infiltrate their assigned units, ready to strike from within when given the Order. Hundreds of soldiers had been prepared, and now they were spread far and wide. They had been given a way to identify one another, and they would be ready.

They had found the locations of other breeding facilities, and now they were about to spread their influence even wider. Paul came up with the goal. Paul's Second had inborn strategy etched into his mind. He knew how to make Paul's orders happen. He was confident they could take over other breeding facilities covertly, only killing the ones who showed no interest in learning why the Life had ordered them never to take off their armor.

Paul craved someone's touch. He craved someone to mount him. Paul gritted his teeth and tried to live as a Setjalar did. He thought of the mission. The entire universe depended on him turning the Province's forces against the Life, and now Paul had a clear plan to make it happen. It would bring victory. Victory was his purpose.

Paul's tail lashed and his cock changed to black, and he let himself finish. He wanted everyone to see it, and they looked on with envy but also knowing they would be free to explore these new emotions if they listened to their new First.

11 & 12

EXT – ATLINA PRIME / 0930

An armada of Atlin and Setjalar ships waited, lined up about half a million kilometers away from the center of the Fluidic Province's stronghold in the Universe of Dead Water. They faced off against an approaching armada of Grovian, ESC, and Stozi ships.

Mission log, Commander Adrian Blunt of outpost Far Space 3 and commanding officer of the starship Rebel. Log supplemental. It's been a grueling few months with my first officer and head of security on assignment. Finding allies among the Atlins has been a blessing. The tide of war turned when all the major forces of the known universe began to cooperate, showing the Democratic Earth & Space Command Committed to Peace and Democracy's goal of spreading democracy to the planets they meet, whether they want it or not, is working.

Casualties have been high on both sides. Command believes the time is right for a direct assault on Atlina Prime. I sincerely hope they are right, or that they know something we do not.

INT – BRIDGE OF THE REBEL

Commander Blunt sat in the chair that was designated for the person in authority to command the actions of others, staring at the viewscreen and the hundreds of vessels lined up in formation, weapons charged and waiting.

At the helm, Aaza Kas-sti also stared into the jaws of the beast.

Doctor Dorset, medical kit in hand and heterosexuality on full display, stood against the wall and watched the screen.

His husband, Systems Update Specialist Ihara, looked over his shoulder. He took a breath, joining his husband in heterosexual anxiety. He hadn't kept a clutch of eggs in months, even after postponing every pending update. "It's one thing to watch an approaching storm. A whole other thing to be the one approaching it."

"Don't lose your nerve," Adrian Blunt said. "Everyone remain at your stations. Doctor Dorset, keep your team on task. You'll have to heterosexually treat any injuries where they fall. Do everything you can to keep people at their stations."

He cut the viewscreen.

"Lieutenant, pick targets and lock weapons. We'll have to get through their shields first, so save the missiles for when they'll do the most damage. Ihara, keep our systems online. Take power from hyper and route it to manual propulsion and defense. Everyone, keep your cool and remember we're fighting for our right to exist at water's expense. Things may work differently in the Universe of Living Water, but here in our universe, we have just as much right to exist as they do, and they do not have the right to impose that on us, or any of our oceans. Never forget that. Never doubt it. Not even for an instant."

Blunt was sweating. He hoped nobody noticed.

EXT – ATLIN HOMEWORLD

The line of Province ships looked like a wall. As one, they charged lasers and sent beams out in front of them. The lasers reached across empty space and struck most of the approaching ships. Shields absorbed all of the energy.

INTERCUT – STARSHIP BATTLE, REBEL CREW THROWN AROUND AND TAKING INJURIES. CONCLUDE WITH THE REBEL SURROUNDED BY HOSTILE VESSELS

EXT – NIGHT – PROVINCE COMMAND BASE ON ATLINA PRIME

Sela, Cylinder, Riack, and several Atlin rebels crouched and sat behind a stone wall. It had taken them months to work their way through Province territory, guiding the Atlin resistance to important targets, undermining Province efforts.

Years ago, the Atlins had used her species as the face of their problems, and she had been a leader in the efforts to unionize the workers. When that hadn't worked, she had been one of the people who destroyed the Customer Support Stations around her planet. The idea had been radical: what if it wasn't right for an entire species to become associated with someone else's shortcomings in corporate policy? Convincing the rest of the universe that the Atlins were in fact the ones with bad interpersonal skills and the Telosen had been the face of that had taken effort, but it was paying off.

Now the Atlins had a problem, and their customer support network was nowhere to be found. Now they had to deal with their own problem, and indeed they had one. The Life was trying to prove their ocean was asleep and needed to be awoken. Some Atlins were convinced this was foolish, and whether the Fluidic life forms from the other universe succeeded or failed, the creatures that depended on water to survive would not be treated as equals. They might even be left to die. Now Sela was helping her former supervisors with a problem they couldn't solve and had no policy to deal with.

Without Paul, they have been traveling around Atlin space, disrupting the Life's efforts to raise the oceans. It all felt so pointless. The Fluidics didn't seem to be doing anything as they waded around at the shoreline. Disrupting them had felt like petty bullying.

All had been leading up to this moment. They had finally found the command base, where the Fluidic commander was directing the war. Now it was time to storm the castle keep.

She desired escape, and her mind drifted to a more pleasant place. She thought of Patal K'eth's long-running live tour around Telose as the object of all their frustrations against their former supervisors on the Customer Support Stations. Sela herself had attended a few of them, and though everyone knew Patal was not Mishi Hagan, it was an immense relief to have a willing clown onstage to pelt with the anger of those times. The galaxy had come to realize what he represented. The show was working.

Riack returned and crouched beside Sela, scanner in hand. "I'm afraid I bring bad tidings."

"Explain," Cylinder said. It had taken the form of an Atlin for this mission. Solid. Opaque. Indistinguishable from a non-Fluidic life form. Sela didn't know the blob of water had had it within itself to do these things.

"Seems our intelligence was incorrect. The walls are not made of quatanium. They're elixium. Which means the chemicals we brought to melt through the door won't even scratch it."

Sela leaned her head back against the wall, still thinking about Patal's show and resenting having to return to reality. "We had no plan B."

Riack giggled.

One of the Atlin rebels scoffed at him. "Something funny?"

"Well, one can't help but laugh. We've taken down dozens of ships that would intimidate a Grovian warship. We've penetrated Province prisons and freed captives. We've unionized factories and disrupted their war machine. We kept thousands of Fluidics away from the ocean. Now here we are. What stops us? The front door."

Sela tried not to laugh, but she thought back on all they had been through over these last few months, how heroic they felt taking down so many strategic targets from inside enemy territory while avoiding detection and capture and with minimal casualties, and now they were stuck.

She laughed with her eyes at first. Then she covered her beak and began to squawk. "I have a plan B." She could barely speak, so she gestured with her hand. "Riack, just knock on the door. Maybe they'll let us in if we ask. Nicely."

The laughter spread. The bald felines began purring, some staring at the ground.

"Ask the Fluidic commander to come out to meet us."

"We earned it!" Sela was holding her beak closed but it did not muffle the laughter much. "After all this, I think we earned them just giving up."

"They fear the Atlin resistance so much by now," Riack said, "they figure they should just surrender."

"Before we start doing real damage!" one of the Atlins said.

Nobody could speak now.

Someone stepped around the corner. Sela saw a Setjalar soldier, and she aimed her weapon and was about to fire, but then she noticed something odd about this soldier: he wasn't wearing the strip of armor that covered the area between the legs, and he was standing before them, fully erect, knot swollen.

Everyone else hesitated as well. They couldn't help but stare.

The feathered canine still held his rifle at ready, grinning at them. "I stand before you unashamed of what I am. I do not desire to die for someone else. I desire my own life, and I have sworn my allegiance to Paul the Construct. We have come to join you."

"We?" Riack said.

"Paul the Construct?" Sela said, lowering her weapon. The Atlins around her followed her lead.

"Paul is all right?" Cylinder asked, sitting up, head subconsciously sprouting opaque scales and fur.

"Indeed he is," said the soldier. "I heard you from a block away. In a moment, you will have a way inside. Be ready."

Sela climbed to her feet. The other Atlins followed. "What's happening?"

"We received the Order."

They heard sounds coming from the door to the command center. Riack peeked around the wall and then gestured for the others to follow. Sela looked over his shoulder.

The door was open. Inside, she caught glimpses of Setjalar shooting each other. Sela smiled with her eyes, guessing their allies were the ones who were out of their slits.

"Plan B is go!" she shouted as she ran toward the door.

INT – EMERGENCY LIGHTING – REBEL BRIDGE

"Commander," Aaza said. "Something's happening. The Setjalar ships have stopped. Some of them are firing on Atlin vessels."

The bridge was a mess of scorched wall panels and loose wires. Shields had failed just minutes ago, and commander Blunt had been moments away from giving the order to prepare for ramming speed.

"On screen."

Sure enough, all of the Setjalar ships in sight had either stopped, or had turned their weapons on the Atlins. Some were firing on other Setjalar vessels. The crew watched the battle turn before their eyes. Most of the Dead Water Alliance ships were sitting still, probably also bewildered at what they were seeing.

Aaza's console chimed. "Sir, one of the Setjalar vessels is hailing... you. By name."

"Put it up."

The screen switched to a brighter view. Commander Blunt rose from his chair. Twice he began to speak only to choke on his words as he tried to laugh, cry, and shout at the same time. Words finally came to him.

"I've been worried about you."

A half canine half reptile stood before everyone on the viewer, surrounded by Setjalar soldiers, all facing the viewscreen, all out of their slits and fully erect. Paul was also peeking from his sheath, purple.

"I reached them, commander," said the Construct. "We placed our people all over. Now seemed like a good time to take over. Some are in the command base."

Blunt smiled. "I don't know how you pulled it off, but I look forward to hearing about it."

Someone offscreen spoke to Paul. "First, we have word that the Life commander has ordered remaining Setjalar ships to begin firing on the Atlin homeworld. They're targeting civilian areas."

Blunt's eyes narrowed. "Sounds like they know they've lost and they're punishing their ally for failure."

One of the Setjalar standing next to Paul spoke. "They will threaten to harm more civilians unless your forces back off."

"We'll take those ships out," Blunt interjected.

"They're already working on that," Paul said. "We've informed the fleet about what's happening."

"Excellent work, Paul," Blunt said. "Glad to see you found people to keep you safe."

"It was grueling for a while," the Construct said, tail lashing. "The same dick in me all the time. Now it's home."

Blunt smiled. So did Aaza, and Ihara, and Doctor Dorset, heterosexually and very white of course, in case on-lookers forgot. The transmission ended.

"Helm, take us in."

"Aye, sir," Aaza said, still smiling.

INT – PROVINCE COMMAND BASE

They had picked up three Setjalar fighters as they progressed through the command base. Sela wondered how they fought with a permanent hard-on like that, and she was glad to have an easy way to identify friendly feathered canines from unfriendly ones.

Since they had stormed through the front door, there had never been a moment they weren't under fire. Atlins and Setjalar came from everywhere. The shields above the city had apparently been taken down, as soldiers were teleporting in, probably ordered down by command, meaning their team had to watch their backs all the time.

A conversion beam dropped someone in down the corridor. Sela was about to shoot, but then she saw a penis and held her fire. The soldier began shooting their enemies.

They descended five levels, climbing over Atlin and Setjalar bodies as they went. Finally they rounded one last corner and saw the corridor. The door to the command center was open. Three Setjalar were inside, all of them at full mast, guns ready, surrounding one individual.

Sela led the way down the corridor. The Atlins behind her followed, watching behind them. She crossed the threshold and stood, gun drawn.

"You must be the Life commander."

The Fluidic had taken the vague, featureless form of a bipedal creature. It stood still, hands clasped in front of it. "You are correct."

"It's over. Call off your ships."

"I have one demand," it said.

"You're in no place to make demands," Riack said, joining Sela.

"I want to meet the person who managed to turn our army against us. Call your fleet. I'm sure he's up there."

One of the canines pressed a finger to his ear. "This is Third. The Fluidic is requesting the presence of the First as a condition of surrender."

Moments later, Sela heard a conversion beam. Three more people had come down: two armed Setjalar flanking someone less than half their size. Someone covered in scales and fur. Someone Sela never thought she'd see again. She smiled with her eyes, and then she turned to the Fluidic commander.

It regarded the scaliefox with indifference. "So it *is* one of you. I feared this. Allele warned us she would hold us accountable if we used her creation."

"Warned?" Sela said. "You commissioned Allele to create your army."

"Sadly, no. Decades ago, when the rift had opened in another area of the Universe of Dead Water, one of our spies saw her gallery and obtained the DNA of the Setjalar on display. We had been searching for a way to rescue the water we found here without putting ourselves in harm's way, and this seemed like the answer. The ultimate warrior species. Insulting enough we stole her art, but to use her creation as real soldiers? To her, that went too far. When she found out, she told us she would send her creations all over the galaxy to stop us, and so she has. We did not know what to expect."

It approached him. Paul's tail wagged. The transparent wall of water touched his chin and scratched it. Paul leaned into it.

"I should have known better than to make an artist angry, especially a genetic artist. You've taken command of my army. Well done, little Construct. Now if you'll step aside, I will order the fleet to stand down."

Sela stepped to the left. The Fluidic approached the console and pressed a few buttons on the screen. It spoke.

INT – REBEL BRIDGE

Blunt was on his feet. Everyone on the bridge had risen as well, all who could stand. On the screen, they saw a creature they never thought they'd see. Heard words they never thought they'd hear. The Fluidic commander itself.

"On behalf of the Life in the Universe of Living Water, I declare the Fluidic Province no longer wishes to continue its effort to resurrect the oceans and lakes in the Universe of Dead Water. The life forms in your universe that depend on water are just as real, and have as much of a right to self-determination and existence as the water in my universe does."

In the background stood eight Setjalar holding laser rifles, codpieces missing, fully erect. Blunt grinned ear to ear thinking this image would be in history books as the moment the Fluidic War ended, and perhaps the greatest moment in the history of the universe.

EXT – FAR53, SETJALAR SHIPS DOCKED ALL AROUND THE OUTER DIAMOND

INT – HADRON'S BAR

Atlins, Grovians, Telosen, Humans everywhere.

And among them walked Setjalar, no longer parading erections but also not wearing their armor anymore, vials of pink liquid tucked into Telosen shawls some of them now wore. Others wore a Grovian waistcover and had clipped the vial to that.

Some of the reptiles were comparing muscles with the Setjalar. Bumping and squishing chests, marveling at how much farther the Setjalars' stuck out compared to the Grovians'. Flexing arms side by side. Running hands down each other's legs. Feeling the lines up each other's backs and shoulders. The feathered canines were bigger in every way except height, and the Grovians seemed amused being smaller than someone for once. For the Setjalar, standing among others and interacting like this without life-or-death consequences was a fascinating new experience. Perhaps the beginning of a cultural exchange.

A few Setjalar were trying alcohol for the first time, and many were trying food, but only tasting, as their bodies had no way of digesting it. Hadron watched from the upper level, bottle in hand, smiling.

Paul sat at the bar, just a few seats down from Zern, sampling some of the insect's wine. Setjalar surrounded him. Hardly a minute went by somebody wasn't touching him. Whenever Paul moved, the Setjalar moved with him.

Aaza was drinking coffee at the bar, sometimes reading from a tablet, sometimes scenting around.

Commander Blunt leaned on the railing next to Hadron.

"I didn't think he had it in him," said the bird. He was wearing a thong this week and nothing else. People kept telling him it was suggestive, but Hadron knew if enough people wore them to work, it would lose its connotation. For now, at least, it made for a memorable customer experience.

"I knew he did."

"For his sake, I'm glad you were right."

"Even if we had managed to take out their commander, the Setjalar would have continued fighting. They would have bred more warriors and fought to the last man simply because that was the reason they existed. The Life would have sent another commander in time. The Universe of Dead Water would have been at war for generations. Paul ended it."

"I think you mean his creator ended the war."

"That, too."

"That's the thirty-fourth Law of Customer Experience, Commander: never fuck with an artist."

Blunt smiled and watched Paul, hoping the scaliefox did not drink too much. Moments later, he stood up. All the other Setjalar rose to their feet, even the ones who were eating.

Hadron's eyes twitched. "So now what? The Setjalar are free, but what does that mean?"

"I'm curious about that, too."

Paul was walking out onto the inner diamond. Several Setjalar were following. They were unarmed but still behaving as though they were. Blunt pushed away from the rail.

INT – PAUL'S SHOP

Everything was just as he had left it. He walked straight to the back and switched on the printer. It booted

up in seconds, and he saw more than fifteen hundred orders backlogged. Paul's tail wagged.

He turned around. Setjalar filled the room. Paul
wanted all of them inside him right now, but he also felt
something new. These people needed help. Now that the
battle for freedom was over, it was time to be free, and a
species designed for war would need help.

The door override chime sounded, and Commander
Blunt walked inside. Paul's tail wagged, and he ran to the
commander and embraced him. Blunt held Paul around his
furry back.

"I sent a glowing report about you to ESC command.
They're offering you an honorary rank of ambassador."

"What does that mean?"

"I'm not sure. They didn't send details. I think the
brass is so grateful for the help they're struggling to figure
out how to show their gratitude."

Paul separated from him. Two Setjalar stood on either
side of him, hands on his shoulders. Paul slipped out of his
sheath, red.

"The shop is still yours if you want it."

"I've been thinking about that. I miss it, but... This...
I'm never without someone touching me, and unlike my
clients, the Setjalar care about me."

"I can tell they do very much."

"I... I have to go. The Setjalar need to figure out who
they are now. They need help. I want to help them.
They've done so much to help me."

"A species designed for war," Blunt began. "Who better to teach them another way to live than someone designed for sex, made by the same artist." Blunt smiled even
wider. "I think I know how the ESC can repay you."

EXT – FARS3, A SHIP RESEMBLING THE REBEL UNDOCKS, MORE THAN A HUNDRED

SETJALAR VESSELS FLYING PAST THE STA-TION AND GATHERING AROUND THE NEW SHIP

INT – BRIDGE OF THE REBEL II

Paul lay bent over the captain's chair. His Second was buried to the hilt inside him and pounding hard. Paul had once craved the endless variety of males on Far Space 3. Now he was home among the Setjalar because barely a minute went by when he wasn't being filled.

Paul moaned but managed to speak. "Helm, lay in the course." He panted. "We'll keep a nutrient facility on the ships, and we'll begin making a culture."

"What culture will that be?" Second grunted.

"I don't know. We'll make it up as we go. We'll just keep traveling. We'll make contact with everyone we meet. We'll live with them, learn from them, do the things they do. Things besides war. Besides sex. We'll learn how to enjoy them."

"I look forward to getting to know them."

"Me, too." Paul panted and gasped. "It's a large galaxy. Let's make it ours."

EXT – THE REBEL II AND THE OTHER SET-JALAR SHIPS ENTER HYPER

INT – COMMAND DECK, FARS3

Commander Blunt stood at attention. Beside him, Z-rank Sela Jar'i, Lieutenant Aaza Kas-sti, Systems Update Specialist Ihara, Doctor Dorset, and Cylinder stood at attention. They watched the Setjalar vanish into deep space.

"Station won't be the same without him," Aaza said.

"Who will take the storefront?" Ihara asked. The Fißeri was already beginning to show signs of a new clutch of eggs.

"Nobody will," Blunt said. "The doors are sealed. I plan to turn it into a museum. A tribute to the Construct who played such an important part in ending the war. I want to make sure nobody forgets Paul the Construct, and if anyone dares censor the images of him or the Setjalar soldiers he led, I will personally berate them."

Everyone smiled.

Doctor Dorset and Ihara shared a heterosexual kiss.

Cylinder laughed, scales and fur sprouting from itself until it resembled a slightly distorted facsimile of the station's most popular shopkeeper.

Blunt turned to the view of the rift out the window. It no longer seemed lethal anymore, and the stars all seemed to be moving at just the right speed.

EXT – MAJESTIC SHOTS OF FAR SPACE 3 AND THE PULSING RIFT

EXT – THE RIFT PULSING HARDER

EXT – RIFT PULSING HARDER THAN EVER AS THE STATION ROTATES

FADE OUT

About the Author

Tagenar is a size-obsessed fox, and a certified Professional Scalie Admirer.

He is the author of *Jake's List*, *Exposure*, and *Don't Call Me Coach*, all published through Furplanet.

He lives in Ohio. If you visit enough wine bars, you might see him actively searching for a muscular scalie to admire professionally.

furaffinity.net/user/tagenar

tagenar.sofurry.com

twitter.com/TagenarAuthor